at

Moosehead Lake

D1520133

Penny Harmon

Christmas

at

Moosehead Lake

Kacey Hammell

About the Author

Penny Harmon began writing at an early age and developed a great love of words over the years. After her children were grown, she took her writing more seriously and has published in both newspapers and magazines. In January of 2016, her first novella, Complicated Inheritance, was published on Kindle. She has also published five books in the Rocky Isle Romance series, with a sixth coming out in March of 2017. A standalone novel, Trying to Forget You, was published in April 2016.

Penny lives in Maine with her long-time partner, Dan, two grandchildren, and three cats. She enjoys spending time with all nine of her grandchildren and enjoys working on DIY projects, especially those of repurposing.

Chapter 1

"We're not married anymore! I don't have to listen to this!" Jenny pressed the release call button and only wished she had one that she could just slam down. It would make her feel better if she could have just smacked him with it instead. Her ex-husband knew what buttons to press and she fell for it every time.

He'd spent the last ten minutes berating her mothering skills and then had the audacity to tell her that he was taking the girls for Christmas, for two whole weeks, and that his girlfriend would be there, too. When she'd objected, he told her that it was in the divorce decree and she had no say whatsoever.

Her girls were just eight and ten and hadn't quite grasped the fact that their parents were divorced. Adding in a girlfriend was not going to do them any good at all. However, after hanging up on him, she realized it would give the girls a chance to see their father in action and perhaps, they'd stop blaming her for everything that had gone wrong. No matter what, though, a call to her lawyer was in order to see if there was anything she could do to stop this infantile behavior from her ex-husband.

Later that night, she explained to the girls that they could either have their Christmas together early or after they got back from their father's. Both girls voted unanimously to have it afterwards and, when she mentioned that their father's girlfriend might be there, they'd both said, "Gross" and they didn't like her already.

She tried to explain to them that his girlfriend had nothing to do with the divorce, although she really wasn't sure of it herself. Either way, the girls let her know that they weren't happy about it.

"I'm gonna punch her in the nose," Andi, her youngest, told her.

"No, you're not. You will treat her with respect," she told her.

Her oldest daughter, Mia, told her, "Well, I'm not listening to her. She's not my mother."

"You need to listen to your father and remember that his girlfriend is an adult."

Both had questioned what she would do for Christmas without them. She told them that she planned on going up to the cabin and would spend her Christmas there.

"Alone?" Andi asked with tears in her eyes.

"You know what? I don't mind being alone once in a while and I can use the extra time to plan a really great Christmas for us when you come home. Plus I'll have Mickey with me."

This had appeased both her daughters, but silently Jenny cursed her ex-husband. She knew their marriage wasn't perfect, but had no idea that he was going to leave. One day, just six months ago, he'd blurted out, "I don't want to be married to you anymore."

Within six months, they were divorced with joint custody of their two daughters and Jenny was left wondering what had happened. Any time she tried to talk to Kevin, he'd simply said, "I just wasn't happy. Deal with it."

She'd dealt with it the best way she could. She was making plenty of money as a self-employed graphic design artist. This allowed her to work from home and put all of the child support she received in the bank for the girl's college fund. She also received a small alimony check each month and she put that toward the mortgage. With any luck, her home would be paid off in ten years.

It was going to be hard, but the two weeks at Christmas without her daughters would be a big test for her. She was planning on using this time to bring back the person she once was…the person she'd once liked. Instead of moping around about spending Christmas alone, she planned on enjoying every second of it. She wasn't going to worry about her daughters. Kevin had been an ass as a husband, but as a father he excelled…usually.

She thought at forty-two that he'd be mature enough to put the kids first, but she'd heard his girlfriend was young and didn't have any kids of her own. Would she be able to handle the two girls that could sometimes be impertinent and sassy? The thought of what could happen actually made her giggle out loud. She felt a little bit guilty, but only hoped that Kevin wouldn't be too rough on the girls should they decide to be insolent.

After tucking the girls in for the night, Jenny went downstairs and got out an old photo album. The pictures were proof of her happy childhood. One showed her sitting on the dock, fishing pole in hand, beside her grandfather. Some considered him a grumpy old man, but he'd been nothing but a big old teddy bear to her.

Another photo was her as a teen, surrounded by about ten others. One was Sherri and she cringed. Even then, Sherri had put her down. It was just sad that she hadn't seen it sooner. She remembered precisely when the picture had been taken. She and Sherri had shopped for hours to find the right bathing suits. It wasn't until Jenny stepped out in front of everyone in hers that Sherri spoke up and told her, "You need boobs if you're going to wear that." She'd never felt so humiliated in her life and, thinking about it now, it only made her more disappointed in her friend.

Closing the photo album, Jenny startled her cat, Mickey, who had curled up on the sofa with her. "Don't worry, Mick. You're going to camp with me."

At fifteen years old, Mickey had been to camp several times with her. It wasn't until after the kids were born that it had become harder. But, Mickey was her pal and there was no way she'd leave him behind this time around. She needed some company after all.

She remembered when she'd brought him home. Kevin had gone ballistic. He'd run around the house screaming, "I can smell the litter box. We don't need some smelly cat ruining our stuff!"

Of course, a few years later when he found out his boss' wife raised Maine Coon cats, he tried changing his tune, but by that point, Mickey had learned to keep his distance and there wasn't any turning back. If only she'd trusted the instinct of her cat, she sighed, but then again, she wouldn't have Mia and Andi, so it was pointless to even think about it.

While she couldn't change the past, she could change her future. The divorce had only been final for a few months, but she'd already noticed some positive changes and not just with her.

It seemed that a lot of her life over the last few years had been spent waiting for Kevin to arrive or doing what he asked of her. He'd call her up at noon and tell her to find a sitter because he'd made dinner reservations with a client and expected her to be there. God forbid if she couldn't find one.

The girls hadn't seen their father much and, if truth be told, they probably saw him more now than they did before. She could also see that they were less stressed…it was hard not to be stressed when Kevin was home.

Shaking her head to get rid of those memories, she looked around the living room. The moment he had walked out with his bags, she'd ripped out the décor, thrown the furniture out onto the lawn, and gone shopping. Her home was now comfortable and the girls loved it. She loved it.

Picking up Mickey, Jenny wandered back upstairs and got ready for bed. Tomorrow would be a busy day as she wanted to email her clients that she would be out of town for two weeks and she would need to finish up the few projects she was currently working on. For the first time in a long time, she was excited about Christmas.

Chapter 2

Two weeks later, Jenny pulled into the narrow drive and smiled when she saw that the plow truck had indeed cleaned up the road so she could get in. There hadn't been a lot of snow yet this year, but if it hadn't been plowed, there is no way she could have made it in. The drive was narrow and long and, while her Explorer had all-wheel drive one small mistake could have left her stranded.

She hadn't been to the camp for almost eight years now and wondered about the condition it was in. Her parents had always had a caretaker, which is who she'd called about plowing the road, but she had no idea whether it had been opened up during this time.

When her father passed away, her mother had refused to come to camp without him. She, being newly divorced, could now understand how her mother had felt. Her now ex-husband had only been to the camp a handful of times, so for her, this was a safe haven...a place of wonderful memories without him.

Pulling up in front of the camp, she smiled. The outside didn't look any worse for wear. Yeah, some of the shingles would need to be replaced soon, but everything basically looked pretty good for a camp that had been abandoned. She only hoped the inside would look half as good.

Preparing to come to the camp for Christmas hadn't been difficult. She was spending it alone and packed only what she wanted. Hamburgers, salad fixings, sandwich stuff, and a few bottles of wine was pretty much what she'd wanted and, of course, she had brought all of the fixings for a Christmas dinner, determined she was going to have a great day.

She'd also brought new bedding because there was no way she was going to be sleeping in mice-infested blankets. And, if there were mice, she only hoped that Mickey would find them first.

Getting out of the Explorer, Jenny stopped and took a breather while she stretched. The four and a half hour ride was something she'd once dreaded, especially when Mia was young and needed frequent bathroom breaks. Poor Andi had never been there since she was an infant. Today, she'd driven straight through with no stops until she got into Greenville.

When she arrived in Greenville, on the southern side of the lake, she stopped at one of the local diners and grabbed some lunch. And, of course, had to hit the trading post because you just couldn't pass it up when you were in the area. These were the things she'd done growing up and it felt good to do it again.

The truth was that she'd been abiding by her now ex-husband's rules for so long that she felt a little funny doing things she enjoyed, but this Christmas was going to focus on her needs and her wants. Her ex got the kids for Christmas this year and she got herself. She was going to make darn sure that she did exactly what she wanted.

Stepping up to the cabin door, she set Mickey down in his carrier and opened the door for him. Then she looked out over Moosehead Lake. This year had been cold and ice had formed on the lake and, after listening to some of the locals in the diner, people were already out snowmobiling and ice fishing on the lake.

She had fond memories of this place and couldn't remember a time when she was younger that she'd missed a trip. Once she was out of diapers, she'd spend two or three weeks every summer with her grandparents. One summer, she'd spent the whole month of July and half of August at camp and cried when she'd had to go home to get ready to go back to school.

Turning back to the cabin, Jenny took a deep breath and unlocked the cabin door. Pushing it inward, she was prepared for the stench of mice, insects, and other potentially nasty critters. What she found stunned her. The place was clean. This was something she did not expect at all.

The refrigerator door was shut and was humming away. When she opened it, she was surprised to find it filled with a few necessities, including milk, creamer, and even a few more bottles of wine.

Wondering what was going on, she was about to give the caretaker a call when she noticed the note on the fridge. It simply said, "Welcome back, Jenny! Merry Christmas!"

With the biggest smile on her face, Jenny danced around the cabin singing Jingle Bell Rock while she started putting her things away. Whoever did this didn't sign their name, but she knew she owed her caretaker big time. She would make sure he got an extra special something right after Christmas...perhaps a gift card to one of the local diners or even the trading post.

Going into the bedroom, she saw the bed was freshly made and Mickey had already found his spot. "Not a mouse turd in sight! How did I get this lucky" she asked herself. After putting the few clothes she'd brought with her away, she wandered back out and started up the woodstove.

Her grandfather had tried to install an oil furnace for her grandmother one time and she'd gone off the deep end. "This is camp! This is not your house! Don't you dare poison this camp with the atrocities of modern times. It's bad enough you put in electricity!" her grandmother had cried.

The woodstove stayed and Jenny, as she started a fire going, couldn't have been any happier. She had many fond memories of that old stove and some not-so-nice ones as well. In fact, she still had a scar just below her elbow of when she got too close as a child.

With the fire raging in the woodstove, the camp heated up quickly. It was a small camp that had been built on a ten acre lot. At one point in their lives, her parents had wanted to build a house on the lake, but like many people, life got in the way and by the time they could have done it, her father had passed away.

Thoughts of her father always made her feel guilty and she sat down in the rocking chair, his favorite in the camp. She'd always been close to her father and mother until Kevin had come along. Her father made no bones about the fact that he didn't like him much, but she was young and in love. What her father thought at that time didn't matter.

Over the years, she hadn't spent a lot of time with her parents and when her father died, the guilt had overtaken her. When she spoke to her mother about it, her mother had told her that her father had understood and not to worry about it. She knew her mother just didn't want her to feel bad.

Since her divorce, she tried spending more time with her mother, but it seemed as though her mother had built a life without her. She had friends and was even going on a cruise this Christmas. She'd pushed her mother away and couldn't blame her. The blame was on her own shoulders.

Her stomach growled and Jenny decided that her first night at camp would be toasted cheese and tomato soup. It was an old camp favorite and one that she didn't normally make for herself at home.

After heating up the soup and grilling a sandwich, Jenny glanced out the window and realized it was snowing. She knew that the weather had stated scattered showers and was happy she'd made it to camp before it started.

Turning on the radio, she hoped to get an update on the storm conditions.

An hour later, after eating and cleaning up the dishes, the weather finally came on and she was shocked to hear that the storm had been upgraded and they were now on a blizzard alert. Smiling, she thought there was no better way to spend Christmas if she couldn't spend it with her girls.

A short time later, Jenny bundled up in her coat, hat, and mittens. Grabbing the hot chocolate she'd made for herself, she stepped outside onto the porch and just stood there watching the snow swirling around her.

This was exactly what she needed...there was nothing that would make your problems seems less intense than realizing just how small you were in the world. The snow was coming down hard and, even though it stung her face, she wasn't ready to go back in. As she sipped her hot chocolate, she watched...occasionally she would see a light across the lake, but as the snow started coming down harder, the light disappeared.

A few minutes later, her nose tingled and she realized that if she stayed out any longer, she'd have frostbite. Back in the cabin, she undressed and added more wood to the fire. The radio was still on and it filled the background with what her ex would consider elevator music.

Sitting down at the kitchen table, she picked up the camp journal and read the last entry made by her:

August 18, 2008

Arrived at 4pm and saw two moose, one deer, and one rabbit on the way up. Stopped in town and picked up some paper plates and saw Old Henry...can't believe he is still around...he must be pushing ninety at least.

Mia is not sure what to think...just toddles around the camp touching everything...and I mean everything. Andi is sleeping in her seat, not even realizing that we've left home. I'm sure she will realize it when she wakes up and screams.

Kevin stayed home to work so it's just me and the girls. Plan on taking them swimming tomorrow just like I did at that age. Until tomorrow.

There was no entry for the next day and Jenny was saddened by the fact that she hadn't filled out the journal the rest of her trip. It would have been nice to remember what they had done before going back home.

Picking up a pen, Jenny wrote:

December 21, 2016

I can't believe that I am back at camp and I'm spending Christmas here. It's snowing, which makes it even better. With any luck, we will get the expected blizzard and it will be perfect!

The girls are with their father for Christmas which means I am here alone, with the exception of Mickey, my cat. It's okay, though. Coming here is like coming home.

The plan for tomorrow is to get out the shovel and clean up some of this snow...coming down hard right now…already have about four inches in just an hour or two.

Until tomorrow!

Jenny turned the pages until she came to the last entry in the journal that her father had made. Her eyes welled up as she read:

July 2, 2010

Moose are out in full force this year. Saw 18 on the ride here. Traffic was heavy. Moosehead Lake is the place everyone wants to be, including the tourists.

Just me and the Mrs. this trip. Jenny off with her new husband. Maybe next time.

Pete

She remembered her father asking her if she and the girls could come up for the holiday and she'd told him next time…that she and Kevin had other plans. If she only knew that there would be no next time…but, she didn't and she still lived with that guilt.

Closing the camp journal, she stood up and walked to the window. The snow was falling harder and there had to be at least a few more inches of snow since the last time she'd looked. With a smile on her face, she stoked the fire before getting ready for bed. Camp meant early to bed and early to rise. There simply wasn't any other way.

Chapter 3

When Jenny woke the next morning, she stretched, forgetting where she was for just a moment. The moment the covers came off, she came to realize she'd forgotten all about the fire. The temperature in the cabin had dropped at least forty degrees and when her feet hit the cold floor, she shrieked, startling the cat and sending him scurrying out into the other room.

Laughing, Jenny threw on her robe and slippers and got the fire started before making herself a pot of coffee. She'd forgotten just how cold the mornings were at camp and thought that maybe her grandfather wasn't so off in thinking a furnace would make it nice. Then she laughed, imagining her grandmother's reaction.

It wasn't long after she had her first cup of coffee that she heard the sound of a plow truck in the distance. Sound carried a long way across the lake, so she wasn't sure exactly how far away it was. A few minutes later, though, she knew it was coming down the road and she hurried to throw clothes on as well as her coat, hat, and gloves.

As she stepped out onto the porch, a black truck with a plow attached came driving around the corner. The driver tooted the horn and maneuvered the truck around the circular drive. She expected it to drive off, but instead, the truck stopped and the driver stepped out.

"Jenny! How are you?"

Jenny couldn't believe her eyes. She hadn't seen their caretaker, Mr. Jones, since she was a teenager.

"I'm great. How are you doing Mr. Jones? I can't thank you enough for coming by to plow and for getting the cabin ready. You did way more than I ever expected and I can't thank you enough."

"Was it okay? I was out of town when you called, so I had Matt take care of it for me. I'll make sure to tell him you said thank you."

"Matt? Oh my gosh! I haven't seen him in years. How is he?" Jenny smiled when she recalled the caretaker's son.

Matt was the life of every party thrown on the lake. Outgoing and friendly, it didn't matter whether you were a local or a tourist...everyone loved Matt, especially the girls.

She recalled the big crush she'd had on him throughout her teenaged years. Without even realizing it, Matt had broken her heart over and over again. Just a few years older than she, he went from girl to girl, but never once did he make a move on her.

Mr. Jones smile revealed a few lost teeth and she remembered how he'd had a tree branch come down on him in the woods...lucky because he survived, which is why these branches were often referred to as widow makers.

"Matt's doing good...lives over yonder across the lake..."

"Do you have time for a cup of coffee? I just made it!"

"Thanks, Missy, but I've got a full load on the truck…I come prepared," he laughed. Then he added in a somber voice, "I was real sorry when I heard your father passed…how's your mother doing?"

"She's doing well…took her a few years, but she's finally living again. I doubt you'll see her back here, though…to many memories, I think."

"Well then, you just give her my best. Oh, we're in for a whopper of a snowstorm later today…I probably won't make it back here for another day or so. I hope that won't be a problem for you," he told her before climbing into the truck.

"Not at all," she was able to respond before his door shut.

The snow was still falling and she wondered how much worse it could get. As Jenny watched him drive away, she suddenly felt lonely. It had been less than twenty-four hours since she'd arrived and now she wondered how she would last for a week.

Grabbing the snow shovel beside the porch, she cleared a path to the woodshed and the doorstep. The snow kept coming down and she could barely tell that she'd shoveled at all.

Figuring it was useless to continue until it stopped, she made several trips to the woodshed to refill the box in the camp. She knew she might not be able to get back out later on that day, so she brought extra in and piled it by the door. At least she would be warm.

Exhausted from shoveling, Jenny sat down at the table and pulled out the camp journal. She wrote:

December 22, 2016

Two more days until Christmas Eve!

Big snowstorm happening right now. We have at least eight inches and a blizzard hitting us later today. Mr. Jones stopped by to plow the drive. Filled the box with wood and brought in extra...just in case! Going to bake a pie later and finish the afghan I've been making Andi. So cold out, but it is beautiful!

Glancing down at the entry, she was happy she didn't make herself sound lonely or pitiful. Not that anyone else would read the camp journal. Her mother refused to come here and all her other relatives were out of state. Times like this made her wish she hadn't been an only child and she could share the camp with someone.

Putting down the journal, Jenny turned on the radio to a station that played Christmas music only and started working on the pie. Her grandmother had taught her how to make pies and, according to anyone that tried them, they were the best.

An hour later, the pie was in the oven and Jenny pulled out the afghan she'd been working on for Andi. With four different pinks, she was sure her daughter was going to love it. Mia, on the other hand, only loved green and she'd finished hers the week before.

It was funny when she thought about her girls. Mia was her tomboy who loved being outside. Andi was the girly-girl and was a princess. The one thing she realized after being back at camp was that she and the girls must make regular visits. Mia would love it.

Thinking of them brought tears to her eyes. She'd never spent more than a weekend away from them since the divorce and, before that, she'd only spent one night away from them and that had been on Kevin's insistence that she attend a convention with him. Of course, when her mother had called and stated that Mia was running a fever, she'd left early which had made Kevin mad.

She was actually shocked that he wanted the girls for the full two weeks. She'd asked if he was taking two weeks off from work to spend with them and got a snort for a reply. His work had always come first and she worried about what would take place if they were left in his girlfriend's care. She'd called her lawyer, but had quickly been informed that according to the divorce decree he could take them for two weeks and choose their childcare provider.

Vowing that she wasn't going to think about it anymore, Jenny put the afghan down and got up to look out the window. It was dark outside and the snow had dropped visibility down enough that she could barely see the lake which was only twenty feet in front of the cabin. Looking to the side, she couldn't even make out the woodshed off to the right and she couldn't imagine having to go back outside in the middle of it. It kind of gave her an eerie feeling...like the feeling that something was about to happen.

Closing the curtain on the window, she threw another log onto the woodstove and set the alarm clock beside the bed to wake her up at midnight so that she could check on the stove again. This was the usual ritual whenever staying at camp in the winter.

Later on that evening, after a small chicken pot pie for dinner, she lay in bed thinking about her time at camp so far. The one thing she loved was that she was on no time line whatsoever. It didn't matter what time she got up or what time she went to bed. She was on her own schedule...which was pretty much non-existent.

She did bring her computer with her and planned on doing some while she was there, but nothing that needed to be done. Part of what she did was creating book covers for self-published authors. She had her own website and always had a bunch of premade covers for authors to select from or they could do a custom made for a little more money.

This was where the majority of her income came from and she'd discovered it completely by accident one day. She'd joined a group on a social site about books and had seen someone else post a premade cover they had made. With her knowledge in graphic design, it was simple. Now she offered covers, webpages, and anything else an author could want to help market themselves. She'd created a niche for herself that was working out wonderful. If only the rest of her life were that simple.

Deciding that nine o'clock wasn't too early for bed, she curled up beside Mickey and was out quickly. It was the first time in a long time that her thoughts did not keep her awake.

Chapter 4

It was just before midnight that Jenny awakened to the sound of whining. It was pitch black in the room and she stumbled to turn on the light switch. She stubbed her toe on the rocking chair and seconds later the alarm clock went off, startling her. She hurried to the alarm clock and shut it off.

Silently creeping out into the main room, she listened closely. Something was scratching on the door of the cabin wanting to come in. The hairs rose on her arms and the back of her neck as she prayed silently for it to go away. If it was a bear, it was obviously going to be a problem because it should be holed up somewhere hibernating for the winter.

The scratching continued and she heard more whining and the more she listened, she realized it sounded more like a dog. As quietly as she could, she went over to the window beside the door in the cabin and switched on the outside light. It was a dog and it was covered in snow.

Grabbing a blanket off the chair, she unlocked the door and cracked it open. If it was a wild dog, which wasn't unheard of in these parts, the last thing she wanted was to give it a chance to attack. However, upon hearing the door open, the dog sat down, wagging its tail, all the while whining to come in.

The dog was a Golden Retriever and its reddish fur was white with snow. It stood up and shook, sending snow flying in through the crack. Jenny laughed and asked, "What are you doing? Did you get lost?"

The dog responded with a bark and another wag of its tail. Sticking her hand out through the crack in the door, the dog lifted its paw in response as if to give her a formal greeting. Laughing, she opened the door a little more and the dog stepped in, allowing her to wipe the snow off with the blanket.

"Where did you come from?" she asked and then laughed at herself because it almost seemed like she was expecting an answer.

Glancing around, she realized that Mickey was still in the bedroom and hoped he'd stay there for now. He'd been around a few dogs before, but she wondered how he'd react to a strange one coming into what he'd now claimed as his own.

The dog, after giving one more shake, walked around and curled up in front of the woodstove. It lifted its head and glanced up at her as if to say thank you.

Reaching down, she lifted the collar to see if there was a tag or any owner's information on it, but only found a tag with the word Minnie on it.

Laughing, she asked the dog, "Are you Minnie?" The dog lifted her head and whined. "Well, now we have Mickey and Minnie. I hope you get along as well as the mice do. You stay here and I'm going to go back to bed after I tend to the fire."

When she opened her eyes again, it was light out and the snow was still falling…not quite as hard, but it was still adding up. Rolling over, she discovered she really couldn't move her feet and discovered Minnie was lying on the end of the bed with her head resting on her feet. What surprised her even more was the Mickey was sleeping peacefully about a foot away. They'd obviously made their own introductions and decided to get along.

"Well good morning! I'm glad you made yourself comfortable," she laughed.

Minnie wagged her tail and Mickey just lifted his head before going back to sleep. "Well, I don't know about you guys," she said, "but I'm hungry."

When she grabbed her robe from the back of the door, both animals watched. Within a few minutes of going into the main room and adding more logs to the fire, Minnie had come out of the room and sat by the door.

"You got to go out? I'll wait for you," she told the dog as the dog went down the steps and did her business just a few feet away from the porch. Within a minute, she was back on the steps and waiting to be let in.

"Hmmm…what am I going to feed you for breakfast? How about some rice, carrots, and chicken?" The dog wagged her tail in response.

After feeding Mickey and Minnie, Jenny put on her outerwear and went outside with Minnie following close behind. She shoveled the path from the cabin to where her Explorer was parked and then the path to the woodshed. Minnie had disappeared, but the moment she was done shoveling, she reappeared and came back inside with her.

Again, she looked at her collar, just to make certain she hadn't missed anything last night. Nothing but the nametag, but she wasn't surprised. Most people forgot to put their own information on their animal's collars and, since she'd done it herself before, she really couldn't hold the owner in contempt.

After cleaning up the camp and washing the floors, Jenny got her computer out of the bag and placed it on the table. Thankfully, she did not need an Internet connection to do any of her work as she'd already saved pictures she would need. Within two hours, she had finished a custom designed book cover for one of her regular clients and had three more premade ready for uploading when she got back to civilization.

Lunch was a quick sandwich and while she ate, she sat down at the table to write in the camp journal:

December 23, 2016

Still snowing! We probably have about 16" already and I'm wondering how much more! I did get a visitor at midnight...a beautiful Golden Retriever showed up on the doorstep covered in snow and cold. Brought her in to get warmed up and she's made herself at home. I wish the girls were here...they would love her. Even my cat Mickey likes her. Got a lot of work done this morning...going to do some more after lunch and get ready for Christmas. I may be alone, but I'm still going to enjoy turkey and all the fixings, and I am going to go out and get a tree to decorate.

As soon as she was done eating, she put the journal away and pulled out her computer to start work on another cover. Suddenly, Minnie stood up and tilted her head toward the door. Within seconds, she was barking.

Jenny stood up and went to the window and not seeing anything, she turned to Minnie and asked, "What's the matter, Minnie?" A minute later, the sound of a snowmobile broke through the silence.

Grabbing her coat and hat, she stepped out on the porch and discovered a snowmobile coming toward her on the frozen lake. Unsure of what was going on, she stood there and waited. When the snowmobile got closer to the edge of the lake, it stopped and the rider, dressed in all black, stepped off the machine and walked toward her.

When the rider took off his helmet, Jenny's heart stopped. This had to be Matt...all grown up. His hair was still the blondish-brown color and close to the style he used to wear it. He had that same prominent chin that stood out and deep, dark eyes. She didn't even realize she was holding her breath until she suddenly felt lightheaded.

"Jenny! How are you? It's me...Matt!" he laughed. "My God! It's been years!"

Jenny took a breath and stated, "I'm good. Merry Christmas!"

By this time, Matt was at the bottom of the steps and looking up at her, his crooked smile revealing white teeth. She couldn't believe that he was standing here in front of her. This is the man that had once haunted her dreams.

"I was just out and about looking for my dog and thought I'd stop in to say hello!"

"Your...dog?" she stuttered.

"Yeah, she went out last night and never came back. She knows her way around the lake, so I'm worried...she should have come back by now."

"Um...I have your dog...she came about midnight and fell asleep by the stove. I'm sorry. I probably should have made her go back outside."

"No. You did the right thing. This snow isn't good and she might have gotten turned around. She was here the other day with me when I was getting the camp ready for you and your family."

"Yes, I meant to say thank you. You didn't have to go to so much trouble. All I was expecting was to be plowed out. You did way more than you should have, but thank you."

Matt laughed. "Believe me, it wasn't a problem. What's it been? Twenty years since we saw each other last?"

Jenny cringed. "Yeah, about that, I guess."

"Well, let me get my dog and I'll get out of you and your family's way," he smiled.

"Oh, it's okay. I'm the only one here," she told him and sighed when he saw the concern in his eyes.

"You're here alone? Didn't you get married and have kids?"

Jenny rolled her eyes. "Yes, I did, but I got divorced and the girls are with their father for Christmas. I came here. It's that simple and no need for you to be concerned. I'm a big girl now."

"I normally wouldn't be concerned, but this storm is going to get worse before it gets better. The winds are supposed to pick up and we're supposed to get a lot of freezing rain."

"That's okay. I have the woodstove and enough wood to get me through."

He ran his fingers through his hair and shook his head. "No, Jenny. We could have trees come down and there are a lot of them right next to the camp that could easily come down on top of it. You can't stay here."

"Um, yeah I can. This isn't the first snowstorm I've been through, Matt. I survived the ice storm of '98, so I don't think this will be a problem."

"Completely different…you weren't here in '98. I was and saw what happened. Trees were down everywhere, including around here. Just take a look behind the camp. Some of those could snap and come right through the roof."

Jenny raised her voice a little. "I don't care. I'm not going home. I'm staying at camp for Christmas."

Matt set his helmet down on the porch and said, "Then I hope you don't mind company, because I'm not going to leave you here alone."

"Um…yes, you are. You have your own family and its Christmas Eve."

"My parents will understand…they won't have a problem with it and I'm divorced…never had kids, so there's nothing to worry about."

Jenny's eyes grew wide. "You are not serious? You are not staying here."

"I'll sleep in front of the woodstove," he laughed, "but you are not staying here by yourself."

Jenny groaned. Still the same old bossy know-it-all, but she was smiling inside. When he'd been a teenager, he'd always been the one that took charge and, obviously, that hadn't changed one bit. The only difference was this teen had turned into a grown man and…a good looking one at that. How the heck was she going to keep her eyes off him?

Chapter 5

An hour later, Jenny was just finishing up another book cover when she heard the snowmobile coming again. She'd tried everything, except for throwing a hissy fit, to get Matt to change his mind about coming back to stay with her. Nothing worked and she doubted that the hissy fit would have either.

Matt had changed a lot over the years, but the one thing he still could lay claim to was his streak of stubbornness. He'd been the same way as a teenager. If he was right, he would fight 'til he won. If he was wrong, it didn't matter.

After he'd left to go pick up a few things at his own place, including some dog food for Minnie, she'd changed into a pair of jeans and a sweater and actually took some time to brush her hair and put on a little bit of makeup. Yeah, she was definitely older and so was he, but he looked more distinguished, while she…well, she still looked younger than her forty years, but she was just starting to show lines around her eyes and her forehead.

When the snowmobile pulled up in front of the cabin, Jenny watched as Minnie pranced around the cabin. At least someone was happy to see him and then she laughed. It would be nice to have some company and at least she wouldn't be eating Christmas dinner alone.

Straightening her hair all over again, Jenny was surprised by the shakiness in her hands and the fluttering in her stomach.

When Matt came through the door, Minnie bounced around his feet until he reached down and petted her. "Did you get lost last night or were you just looking for some new company?"

Minnie whined and rubbed around his legs, clearly happy to see him. Mickey must have wondered what the ruckus was because he slinked out of the bedroom and hopped up onto the chair. Within seconds, Minnie was trying to crawl up in the chair beside him. After a moment, he moved over just enough that gave her enough room to maneuver herself around.

"Well, I see Minnie found a friend," Matt laughed.

Jenny laughed and told him, "Oh yes! Mickey and Minnie have become fast friends!"

Matt's mouth hung open. "Mickey and Minnie? Seriously?"

The laugh that came out of Jenny's mouth surprised even herself. "It must be fate. They've been inseparable since Minnie arrived...even slept together at the foot of my bed last night."

"Well, that's a surprise since all Minnie has ever done is chase cats. I'm shocked...it must be your cat or something."

Jenny watched as Mickey moved around the dog and found enough space to lie down. He closed his eyes after sending a glance their way, as if to say, "Okay...shows over so quiet down."

Matt looked at her and grinned and she could have sworn her heart skipped a beat. He seemed to have the same hold over that he had when they were teenagers running around the lake. She would have done just about anything he'd asked back then and she told herself she wasn't about to be that same lovesick girl again…ever again. It just wasn't worth it.

A few hours later, as they were reminiscing about their summers on the lake, the power went out. Matt looked at her gravely and said, "I'm surprised the power has stayed on this long. Do you have a generator? I didn't see one when I was here before."

"Um…no. My grandmother forbid it. We're lucky to have power at all. She was certainly set in her ways and was dead set against it."

Chuckling, Matt told her, "I remember your grandmother all too well. I remember the summer I started hanging around. It wasn't long before she was warning me away…told me you might have looked older, but you were way too young for me. I didn't dare look your way again."

"What? My grandmother did that?" Jenny was shocked. Her grandmother hadn't said a word to her about anything.

"Oh yeah she did! Scared the living daylights out of me!"

Jenny shook her head. "Is that why you ignored me so much?"

Matt nodded his head.

"I thought you hated me or something or thought I had cooties or something," she laughed. Deep down she was thrilled that there was a reason he never paid attention to her as a teenager.

"Hated you? Heck, I had the biggest crush on you, but I wasn't messing with your grandmother," he snorted.

Jenny could only laugh. Her grandmother had been five feet tall at one point, but due to old age, she'd shrunk at least two inches over the years. She might have weighed eighty pounds and only if she was soaking wet. The thought of Matt being scared of her was actually quite comical.

Suddenly, Jenny thought of something. "Oh my God! We don't have power. How am I going to cook?"

"Probably won't get it back for days, either. We don't need power...we have the woodstove!" Matt responded without worry.

Jenny looked at him like he'd grown three heads. "The woodstove? I can't cook on that thing."

"Why not?"

"Because...because I need a stove...an actual oven," she stammered.

Matt stood up and opened up the door on the right-hand side of the woodstove. It was a little dusty inside, but the heat coming out was immense. "What do you think this is?" he asked.

"Not the kind of oven I need. I need one that has a temperature gauge...I can't imagine using that," she gasped.

Matt gave her a look that conveyed his amusement. "Well, it is hot, but not too hot. What are you planning on cooking?"

"A turkey, you fool! Christmas is all about turkey! I planned on cooking a small one...well, not a whole turkey, but turkey breasts with stuffing and the works." Her exasperation showed in her voice and she instantly regretted it when she saw his eyebrows rise.

"I have an idea. Why don't we go to my house? I have a generator," he smiled.

She knew that it was a great idea, but the thought of going out in this weather wasn't ideal to her and she'd have to leave her cat behind. Shrugging her shoulders, she stated, "I can't leave Mickey behind and, even if you told me to bring him, I couldn't because it would be too much for him."

Glancing over at Mickey and Minnie, Matt gave her a grin. "It looks like we're going to have to learn how to cook in this thing then. I'm game if you are?"

Jenny couldn't help the smile that spread across her face. If her grandmother could do it, so could she. After lighting some lanterns around the cabin, she sat down in one of the chairs and told him, "Well, it's a good thing I made the pie yesterday…otherwise I might be in trouble."

"Pie? What kind of pie?" Matt asked with overly exaggerated interest.

"Apple, but I didn't say you could have any," she laughed and then realized it sounded like she was flirting with him. Was she? It had been years since she'd done any flirting with anyone and it felt kind of good.

"Hmmm…if you want to play that way, then I'm not going to show you how to use this oven," he teased.

"If you don't show me how to use the oven, then I can't…or won't make you a turkey dinner for Christmas."

Suddenly, a loud crash shook the cabin. Leaping across the room, he grabbed Jenny and pulled her away from the window. Minnie had jumped off the chair and stood in front of them wagging her tail and barking. Mickey jumped out of the chair and into the other room where she assumed he took safe haven under the bed.

Matt's arms were still around her and Jenny felt the heat coming from him. He smelled of the outdoors…of wood…of smoke…it was every scent she ever thought of as being sexy

54

and she couldn't believe she was standing there in this man's arms. When Minnie barked, however, it broke the spell he was holding on her and she stepped back.

"I think you were right about those trees. I think we just lost one."

Stepping to the back window, he told her, "Stay inside. I'm going to get a light and check it out. Keep Minnie in here, though. I don't want her to get hurt if it's not done falling yet."

"I'm going with you. I want to see if there is any damage."

The look on his face told her that he wanted to argue, but finally, he shrugged his shoulders and told her to dress warmly. A few minutes later, they were staring at the tree while ice pelted them in their faces.

The tree had come down within just a few feet of the cabin. At two feet in diameter, it would have done significant damage if it had hit the cabin and Jenny shivered. She forgot how dangerous it could be in the middle of a snowstorm and was thankful that Matt was with her.

Grabbing his arm, she turned to tell him that they could wait to clean it up tomorrow when another crash sounded nearby. Another tree was coming down and he pulled her with him as he ran back to the steps of the cabin.

"We have to stay inside. It's getting dangerous out here," he told her.

Jenny could feel the tremors in her body and her knees were weak, but she didn't know if it was the adrenaline rush of the falling tree or the fact that he held her so close. Putting her head down on his chest, she took a deep breath.

"Did I tell you how glad I am that you insisted on staying? I don't know what I'd be doing right now." When she looked up at him, he was looking down at her with concern.

"Are you okay?" he whispered.

Fearing she was making a fool out of herself, she stepped back and nodded her head. She regretted her decision the minute that she did.

"Let's just get inside where it's safe…well, a little safer." Stomping the snow of their boots, they entered the cabin and pulled off their coats and boots.

He looked at her and stated, "I wish like hell I had convinced you to go to my place. It's a lot safer there, but it's too late now...we're stuck here until this is over."

Jenny wasn't sure whether she should laugh or cry. Instead, she went over to the chair where the animals were curled up together and leaned down to pat them...anything to keep her eyes and her mind off from him.

Chapter 6

As Matt added wood to the fire, Jenny opened the fridge and took out some sandwich meat. She wasn't about to test the woodstove yet and figured that some ham and cheese sandwiches would be the perfect choice. She even pulled out a container of her homemade chicken soup to go with it.

He watched her as she poured the soup into a pan and placed it on the stove. When she looked at him, she could see the smirk on his face. "You got something to say?" she asked.

"Um…no, but I do have a question for you. Thought you didn't know how to cook on a woodstove?"

She tried to hide the grin on her face and smacked him in the arm. "Um, it's just soup, not a freaking turkey!"

"Well, I think we'll do just fine with the turkey! I can't wait." He rubbed his hands together as if he couldn't wait to get his hands on the turkey and she turned away quickly. This was just getting to be too much fun for her and for the first time in a long time, she was actually laughing with a man.

After she put the food on the table, Matt sat down beside her and picked up the camp journal in front of him. "What a great idea! I love the fact that you actually record your trips."

She watched as he scanned through the entries. It wasn't like she was embarrassed by what she wrote, but still it was personal to her. She felt instant relief when he put it down.

"So, what made you decide to come back to camp after all these years?"

Jenny didn't know why she was suddenly shy about her answer, but she did know that her reasons for coming were personal. She didn't know if she was ready to share that with him just yet...if ever. She simply answered, "I thought it would be fun."

Matt's eyebrows rose. "Fun? In the middle of winter?"

Seriously? He was going to question her reason? "Yes, Matt. I thought it would be fun to come back to camp. I haven't been in too long, so…when I realized I'd be alone, I thought it would be perfect."

Chuckling, Matt told her, "You know what? You're right. This is fun, even if you don't know how to cook on a woodstove."

Picking up the cap to his water bottle, she threw it at him. All she could think was this is what it was supposed to be like with a man…laughing…having fun…not worried about whether or not everything was perfect.

She'd married Kevin right out of high school and, while she did finish college, she'd always put his career as a lawyer ahead of her own. The truth was that Kevin had always made the rules and she'd simply followed along.

Christmas time was always about who decorated their house the best…everything had to be the top of the line and, quite often, Jenny herself didn't live up to his expectations of perfection.

When they'd first split up, it had been hard to make decisions, but over the last few months, she'd proven to herself that she was not as dumb as Kevin had tried to make her feel.

Jenny also realized that she had a lot to offer someone. She wasn't exactly the skinny girl she used to be, but after having children, she had curves where she'd never had them and she at least now needed a bra. Before children, she never had to wear one and just knowing that she had a little more up top gave her a little more confidence.

She knew it wasn't good to be so vain, but over the years of her marriage, she'd been put down more than she'd been complimented. It wasn't as if she needed a compliment every second of the day, but when they dressed up to go out to dinner, it would have been nice.

Over the last six months, she'd held herself accountable for everything she did. It was a very powerful feeling to know that she was finally in control of her destiny. While most of her friends had congratulated on her new found confidence, she had a few that didn't like it.

One friend in particular had hurt her deeply. She and Sherri had been friends since first grade and Sherri had spent many summers with her at the camp on Moosehead Lake. However, Sherri lived off other people's insecurities. She didn't mean to be like that…this Jenny knew…but she was the type who had to put others down to make herself look better.

When Kevin had walked out on her, Sherri had almost seemed happy that she was miserable. When Jenny lost the extra ten pounds, Sherri told her she looked anorexic. When Jenny told her she was happy, Sherri had told her that she heard Kevin had cheated on her throughout her whole marriage.

After a lot of soul searching, Jenny came to the conclusion that she could no longer be friends with Sherri. Very bluntly, she'd told her she was removing toxic relationships from her life and wished her well. Sherri had huffed and puffed, but walked away, stating that Jenny had changed and she didn't like who she'd become. Jenny had walked away with a smile on her face.

Sherri had been one of her friends that used to hang all over Matt and, the thought of what her friend would do now if she could see her at camp with Matt made her smile. If only...she stifled a giggle and took a quick glance at Matt.

He, of course, was still eating, fumbling through the camp journal, reading some of the older entries, and thankfully hadn't noticed her ogling him. Grabbing her empty bowl of soup, Jenny took it over and rinsed it out using a ladle full of water from the bucket on the top. Once he was done, she rinsed out his dishes and then poured them each a glass of wine.

Sitting back down at the kitchen table, Jenny sighed. It was only eight o'clock, but it felt much later. Of course, she was used to going to bed this time of night. Her girls were early risers, something they definitely didn't get from her.

Matt got up and walked over to the bookcase and pulled down the Monopoly game sitting on the top shelf. "All the pieces here?" he asked and she couldn't help but notice the gleam in his eyes.

"Last I knew they were, but look at the dust. I don't think it's been played in years," she laughed.

Taking a deep breath, Matt let it out quickly, sending dust flying in all directions, which dissolved him into a fit of coughing and Jenny into another fit of the giggles. Matt overdramatized it all, which made it even funnier.

A half hour later, Jenny realized just how competitive Matt was when she landed on Park Place and he let out a whoop of joy.

"Yes, hand it over quickly, my Dear. Time's wasting and I have more property to purchase!" he grinned.

She felt his smile all the way down to his toes and, as he took the time to pour her another glass of wine she realized that she was feeling a little tipsy. The giggles that were coming out of her couldn't be just from her happiness, could they? It had been so long that she'd had this much fun that she wasn't sure whether it was alcohol-induced or not.

The funny thing was that she didn't care. If Kevin had been around, he'd probably be whispering in her ear that she was making a fool of herself. The thought sobered her for a moment, but looking across the table at Matt, she didn't care. This wasn't Kevin's life…it was hers…and she was determined to have some fun.

Another glass of wine later, Matt was well on his way to holding all of the money. A meager two hundred dollars and holdings to a railroad and three properties were all that she possessed. Matt watched her carefully as she prepared rolled the dice.

Holding her breath, she shook them in her hand and then brought her hands to her mouth. Her lips parted and she gave them a kiss before dropping them onto the table. Her eyes came up and she noticed Matt's eyes. They were no longer looking at the dice…they were looking at her…her lips to be precise. As her heart beat faster, her breath quickened.

Matt leaned forward in his seat and...SNAP...another tree came down just outside the camp sending them both to their feet and Minnie into another barking frenzy.

Matt grabbed his coat. "Stay here. I mean it!" As he opened the door, all she could think was that she didn't have much of choice because the look he'd been giving her had taken the breath right from her and she didn't think she was capable of actually walking.

Standing there in shock, Jenny took a deep breath. What if the tree hadn't fallen? Would he have actually kissed her? What would she have done if he had? The thought sent shivers down her spine and left her numb with cold.

She'd come here to Moosehead Lake to work...to take her mind off her first Christmas without her girls...not to find a man! The thought of what she'd almost done scared her. The last thing she needed was to make another mistake!

Sitting back down, she looked at the wine. The bottle was gone...only a drop or two left in her glass. Oh my God! She was making a fool out of herself. When was the last time she'd drank a full bottle of wine? Matt had only drank a glass and a half.

Standing up on shaky legs, she walked over to the window and looked out. It looked like the snow and ice had stopped...although who knew for how long. The weather report had stated it could go on like this for two more days.

Hearing Matt's footsteps on the porch, she stepped back to give him room to get in. Snow covered his boots and he stomped them onto the rug, while taking off his coat.

"This one was close, but hopefully where it's let up, there won't be any more coming down tonight...unless the wind picks up. I'll have to go get my chainsaw in the morning and clean up some of the mess," he told her while hanging his jacket onto the back of the chair.

"Um, yeah...you don't have to go to all that trouble, Matt. I'll have someone get in and clean it up later." Turning around, she went back to the table and picked up her wine glass to empty it out into the sink. "Not a big deal if it waits until spring."

Matt's eyes followed her. "Everything okay?" he asked.

"Yeah, the tree coming down just startled me is all. I just don't want you going to any trouble over a tree. I've already been a bother already," she told him. "You know, why don't you go with your family to dinner as planned. I've got work to do, so really, it's no problem."

Jenny took the plates from their dinner and stacked them by the sink. Her hands shook and she did everything, including counting to ten and taking a deep breath to stop them. It wasn't working.

Matt's voice startled her, "Jenny, if I made you uncomfortable, I'm sorry. We were having a lot of fun and, well, I wanted to kiss you. That's all. I promise you're safe with me."

Feeling her breath catch in her throat, Jenny gasped. "Um...no, it's all good. Honestly...I just...I really do have a lot of work to do. That's all."

Laughing, Matt came up to her and put his hand on her shoulder and she instantly felt the heat. "It's okay. You deserve some time off. We're going to have fun!"

Nodding her head, she didn't dare to look at him. When he finally removed his hand from her shoulder, she was able to let out the breath she'd been holding.

Chapter 7

Jenny pulled the covers up to her chin and let out a sigh. This was the first time in six months that she'd slept with a man in the same house. Granted, this one was out sleeping on the bunkbed in the main room, but…it was weird. Plain as that…it was weird.

Every sound he made seemed to echo throughout the cabin and she wondered if he could hear every sound she made. In turn, this made her self-conscious about everything, including her breathing.

After Matt insisted on spending the day with her tomorrow, as well as eating Christmas dinner with her, he'd yawned and told her he'd take Minnie out one more time before bed. She hadn't wasted anytime in getting ready while he was out, thankful for the outhouse that her father had attached to the camp. Emptying the bucket was certainly no fun, but it beat going outside in this type of weather.

By the time Matt came back in, Jenny had put on her pajamas, her robe, and her rabbit-eared slippers. She didn't expect the chuckle that came out of his mouth when he saw her, but what was she supposed to wear? It was the only thing she brought and she wasn't exactly expecting company.

The snores coming from the main room were not expected, but she did find them comforting. What seemed like moments later, she was awakened by the sound of Minnie dancing around the main cabin and the voice of Matt whispering at her to be quiet. The door opened and shut and then silence. Glancing at the clock, she saw it was seven and sighed.

Not enough sleep, but once she was awake there was no returning. This was the problem she had when her girls were younger. If they woke her up at four in the morning to use the bathroom, she ended up staying up, knowing she'd never go back to sleep.

Slipping on her robe and her slippers, she walked out of the bedroom and into a warm main room. The smell of fresh coffee hit her and she grinned. Going over to the pot, she poured a cup for each of them, leaving his black as she had no clue what he put in his.

When she heard his footsteps on the porch, she set both cups down on the table and sat down in one of the chairs. Smiling, she watched as Minnie came bounding in the door and straight to her.

"Good morning, Miss Minnie! Did you have a good walk?" she murmured while stroking her head.

Matt growled. "Well, it's no longer freezing rain, but damn, it's cold outside."

"I poured you a cup of coffee," she said.

After taking off his boots, he walked over to the table and sat down beside her. "What's on your agenda for today? It's Christmas Eve, you know?"

The laugh escaped her lips before she could stop it and she looked at him in anticipation. "A tree? Is that too much to ask?"

Smiling, he whispered, "A tree? You can't have Christmas without one!"

Taking a sip of coffee, she sat back in her chair. "Do you have a phone at your house? Or do you think it's out, too?"

He shook his head. "No, I only have my cell phone. Yours isn't working?"

"No reception here."

"Well, feel free to use mine anytime you want."

"Thanks. I wanted to give my girls a call...it's my first Christmas without them."

"What happened that he got them for Christmas?"

Shaking her head, she whispered, "I...uh...we're taking turns. Next Christmas is mine."

"That doesn't make it any easier, though...next Christmas is a long ways away."

Feeling the tears well up in her eyes, she stood up and said, "Well, I better get dressed and figure out something to feed you so we can go tree hunting. Give me a few minutes."

In the bedroom, she chided herself for being so weak. She knew this was going to happen and...well...she still wasn't prepared for it. Christmas without the girls was just...well...it sucked to put it mildly.

Throwing on a pair of jeans and a sweater, she ran a brush through her unruly auburn hair and glanced at herself in the mirror. Rolling her eyes at her reflection, she didn't even know why it mattered. What would he even see in her?

Back in the kitchen, Matt had taken the lead and had thrown some eggs in a frying pan on the stove and had placed some bread on a rack that he was putting inside the woodstove's oven.

"What are you doing? I told you I'd make you breakfast," she stated. "You didn't have to do this."

Matt laughed. "I like to cook. In fact, I consider myself a pretty good cook. Wait 'til you try the eggs!"

"What can I do?" she asked. She was not used to being waited on and stood beside him wondering what was left to be done.

"Just go sit and have a second cup of coffee. How many mornings do you get to just relax?"

Sitting down, she told him, "Honestly, none. The girls are morning people, so they are up early and raring to go before I can even open my eyes."

"Tell me about them," he told her. "They sound sweet."

"Oh, wow! Where do I begin?" she laughed. "Mia is the oldest. She's ten and she's something else. She's at that stage where she doesn't know if she wants to be a little girl or a preteen. Does something and then yells at her sister for doing the same thing and calls her a baby. I don't get it."

Matt's laughter filled the room as he pulled the toast out of the oven and put the eggs on plates for each. Setting them down on the table, he told her, "It's a tough age to be. I wanted to do everything my father did, but I wasn't ready to give up my matchboxes either."

"Yeah, she's a great kid, though. Andi is eight and she's my girly-girl…loves pink…loves ballet…and has the biggest heart."

"They sound perfect. I have two nieces that are about that age and they can be a handful," he chuckled. "Drives their mother nuts, especially now that the oldest one has discovered boys. She's eleven."

Jenny shrieked, "Bite your tongue. Mia is nowhere near ready to like boys yet. Oh my God, I hope not anyway."

Taking the first bite of eggs, Jenny groaned. "What did you do to these eggs?"

"I'd have to kill you if I told you," he whispered with a grin and lit up eyes.

Taking another bite, she grinned. "I know there are chives."

"Well, that's the easy one," he teased. "Tell me what else."

"Um…let me see," she whispered. Placing another bite of eggs into her mouth, she took her time. "Basil?"

"Yes, but that's another easy one. What else? Come on. Think about what your tongue is telling you. What does it taste like? How does it feel?"

"It's creamier than what my scrambled eggs usually are...it has almost a sour taste, but it also tastes tangy..."

"You're getting there. Take another taste," he told her and leaned closer.

Another bite of the delicate eggs went into her mouth, but she couldn't take her eyes off from his. The look of eagerness on his face was a little more than she could take and she swallowed the bite quickly.

"Um, I don't know, but whatever it is, these are the best scrambled eggs I ever had," she mumbled and took another bite.

Leaning back, he laughed and shook his head. "You gave up way too easy. It's just mayonnaise and cream cheese. I hope you weren't going to use the cream cheese for anything special."

His laughter was contagious and soon she was laughing with him. "Yeah, you big goof! I was going to use those with the mashed potatoes for Christmas dinner. Now, your mashed potatoes are going to be plain and boring!"

"No way. I have some cream cheese at my house. When we go out to get the tree, we can stop by and grab it and see what else we can find. I have to contribute something, you know."

"Oh, you're going to be in charge of the turkey," she demanded with a grin.

"Really? You trust me with it?"

"I don't, but I will still let you do it," she laughed.

"Okay, then. Finish those eggs now, young lady. Then we're going out to find the most beautiful tree on Moosehead Lake."

In less than a minute, the eggs and toast were history and they were getting dressed to go outside. Donning a pair of an old pair of snow pants that were hanging in the closet and her coat, she then wrapped a fluffy pink scarf around her head. At least she would be warm.

Matt had put on his snow gear and waited by the door. "You ready? Mickey and Minnie we will return...if we don't freeze our butts off first!"

Chapter 8

Jenny couldn't see where she was going, but she felt great. Her arms were wrapped tightly around Matt in front of her and the wind whipped all around her. The helmet was snug and, while she was a little chilly, it wasn't anything she couldn't handle.

The lake had frozen early this year due to the extremely cold temps and they whizzed across the lake quickly. As they slowed down and stopped, she wiped the front of the helmet to get a better view and then slipped it off.

A log cabin stood in front of her on a small sloping area. On the front was a large porch and there was an entry door on the bottom going into the basement. A small shed stood off to the side that matched the exterior of the log home.

"Well, this is home," Matt stated.

"It's beautiful, Matt. How long have you lived here?"

"Well, I just put this up a few years ago, but I've owned the land for about ten. There used to be a small camp, but well...I wanted something bigger."

"I love it!" she told him.

"Well, come on in then...wait 'til you see the rest," he laughed.

After walking in through the basement door, they both sat down on a log bench and removed their outerwear. The basement entrance was huge and she was instantly jealous of the space. A large closet lined one wall, a boot rack lined the other, and the third held the bench where they sat.

Where it opened up, she could see a large family room with the largest fireplace she'd ever seen. Standing up, she tiptoed over to the doorway and gasped. The whole interior was done in natural logs and, while there weren't many windows, it was light and airy.

"You like it?" Matt said as he came up and stood directly behind her.

Turning her head around to look at him, she said, "How could I not?"

As he grabbed her hand in his, he pulled her into the open room where she noticed two doors toward the back of the room. He nodded and told her, "An extra bedroom and a bathroom, but the real kicker is this." He let go of her hand and pointed to the side.

A huge tree trunk, which seemed to come right out of the cement floor, stood in the back corner. The top had been cut flat and it was varnished. About three feet across, it was something that could never be duplicated and made the perfect table near the bar.

Running over to it, she ran her hands over the smooth top and down its side. "How? This is magnificent!"

Coming up to stand beside her, he shrugged his shoulders. "Let's just say a lot of hard work was involved and a lot of time."

"You did this?" She was amazed. Something like this would go for thousands of dollars in the city.

"Yeah, the tree won...would have cost me a lot more to have it hauled out. Instead of fighting it, I chose to work with it and this is the end result."

"It's breathtaking. I thought the fireplace was the focus piece, but I was wrong," she laughed. "I can't wait to see what is upstairs if it's anything like this."

Again, Matt grabbed her hand and started pulling her toward the staircase off to the side. This, too, was a stunning piece with handrails made out of wood branches that had been sanded to perfection.

At the top of the stairs, she stopped and looked around. There was nothing common about this place. She'd been in many log cabins in her lifetime, but this was the most creative she'd ever seen. With more branches highlighting entryways and tree burls as pieces of art, it was nothing like she'd ever seen.

"I don't know where to look first," she whispered. "This is...I don't know...the word amazing really doesn't justify it well enough."

"Well, thank you. I like it. Took me almost three years to finish and I've grown a little partial to it."

Standing in the main room, she couldn't help but keep looking at his handy work. She couldn't imagine having this type of talent.

"So, besides the cream cheese, what else do we need?" he asked from the kitchen.

"Um, it's up to you! I'm not a fancy cook...not like you are," she laughed.

"Fancy? No. I just like to eat good food," he replied. "How about some roasted Brussel sprouts to go with dinner?"

"Sounds good," she smiled. If someone had told her twenty-five years ago that someday she'd be standing in a kitchen with Matt picking out side dishes for Christmas dinner, she would have thought they were crazy.

After filling up a grocery bag with various items, Matt told her to wait inside while he got some things out of his shed.

On the mantle over the fireplace, which wasn't quite as large as the one downstairs, she looked at the pictures displayed in frames. One was of him and his parents, with his sister sitting beside him. Another was of two young girls, who must be his nieces. Another was a picture of him and an article from the local paper that stated, "Local artist featured in *Art in America*!"

Before she could read the clipping, she heard Matt come through the door downstairs. She yelled, "I didn't know you were an artist!"

She heard his chuckle and then he yelled, "You didn't ask!"

Grinning, she looked around and sighed. This was amazing. She'd had no clue when they were teenagers that Matt would turn into someone famous. She didn't know much about art, but she knew that to be featured in *Art in America* you had to be someone pretty special.

When he came up the steps of the stairs, he asked, "What do you do for a living?"

"Um…graphic designer…mostly book covers and that sort of thing."

"So, you are an artist, too." It wasn't a question, but rather a statement.

"Um, not of your caliber, I'm not," she laughed. "I just manipulate things on the computer."

"Not as easy as it sounds, I'm sure," he said. "I couldn't do it. I work outside mostly…with wood, obviously," he laughed while looking around.

"Did you always do this type of thing? I mean, I had no idea what you liked or didn't like when we were teenagers. I just worshipped you from afar," she laughed and then realized what she said and felt the heat rising in her face.

His gaze fell on her and she quickly looked away. Could she be any more brazen? She couldn't believe she'd just told him she'd worshipped him when they were kids. What was she thinking?

"Come on, Woman. I have the sled packed up. We're about to go on an adventure!" he yelled while clapping his hands together. "Let's get a move on!"

Laughing, she forgot all about her embarrassment and followed him downstairs to put their outerwear on again. Suddenly, she realized she forgot to call her girls.

"Oh my God! I almost forgot. Can I use your phone?" she gasped. "I need to call the girls."

Smiling, he took his phone out of his pocket and handed it to her. "Go in and sit by the fireplace while you talk to them. I'll wait here."

Sitting down on the suede sofa, she dialed her ex-husband's number and soon heard his voice on the other end.

"Hi Kevin. Sorry, my phone doesn't work up here. How are the girls?"

"Jennifer. They are good. Is there a problem?"

"Um, no. I was just hoping to say hi to them. I miss them," she said.

"Well, they are out shopping right now. Do you want to call back later?"

Hesitating, she told him, "I will do my best, but it depends on reception. Tell them I love them and, if I don't call later, I will try them tomorrow."

"Yeah, I'll tell them," Kevin said and promptly hung up on her.

When she handed the phone back to Matt, he'd looked at her and asked, "Are you okay?"

She'd wiped the tears away and didn't want to start in again, so she simply smiled and said, "Let's get this show on the road!"

Chapter 9

An hour later, Jenny was exhausted. It was just after lunchtime and they were now traipsing through the woods in search of the perfect tree. When she'd picked one out earlier, Matt had stated, "That is not a tree...it is a stick with a few needles sticking to it. You need something better than that!"

"No, come on," she told him. "It will be cute."

"Thou shalt not have an ugly Christmas tree," he demanded, making her laugh.

"Fine...than you choose one!" she replied and stomped off down the path with a smile on her face.

It wasn't long before Matt had caught up to her and pointed in the woods beside her. The spruce tree was small, only about four feet high, and had thick branches sticking out in all directions. "With a little trim here and there, it will be perfect," she laughed. "I love it!"

As they rode back to camp on the snowmobile with the sled behind them, her mind wandered back to her conversation with Kevin. Were the girls really shopping or was he just trying to prevent her from talking to them? And, if they were shopping, was it with his new girlfriend?

She didn't want to deprive them of time with their father, but the thought of him bringing another woman into their lives bothered her. Was it too soon or was it just her? Was she jealous? She really didn't think she was jealous; she had recently discovered how much happier she was without him.

Her thoughts were interrupted when the snowmobile hit a bump and sent her up in the air. Laughing, she squeezed him harder. Matt pulled the sled over anyone to check on her.

"You okay?" he yelled so she could hear him over the engine.

"I'm great! That was fun!" she laughed.

"Hold on tight," he roared.

Across the lake they sped, her laughter dying in the wind. She hadn't had this much fun in so long. When she was a kid, she'd come up here and ride around on her father's snowmobile with the other kids on the lake, but never like this…never feeling so free…so alive.

She was disappointed when they pulled up to her cabin and ruefully pulled off the helmet when they came to a stop.

"That was so much fun! I can't believe I forgot how much fun snowmobiling can be!"

"Well, around here, I mostly use it as a mode of transportation when the weather is rough, but…yeah, it can be a lot of fun. Maybe tomorrow we can go for a ride after dinner," he suggested.

Standing up, she looked at the cabin with the smoke still coming out of the chimney. How did she get by without coming back here for so long?

"That would be great," she told him. "Now, let's unpack and I'll make us some sandwiches for lunch."

Sitting down at the table, they both wolfed down the ham and cheese sandwiches she had made, each with a glass of soda. She didn't drink a lot of soda, but because it had reminded her of camp when she was getting ready to go, she'd brought it with her.

"Where are you going to put the tree? In the corner?" he asked in between bites.

"Yeah, that's where we usually put it up. Plus, there is an outlet right behind it." Then she laughed, "Never mind. I forgot we don't have power."

"That's okay. I brought some battery operated lights back with us."

"What a great idea," she told him and then silently ate the rest of her sandwich. Granted, she never really dated much before Kevin and hadn't dated at all since her divorce. But, in her eyes, either Matt was going out of his way to impress or he really was just a thoughtful guy. She just hadn't decided which...yet.

Before Matt went outside to get the tree, he put some new batteries in the radio and tuned it in to local station that only played Christmas music. It wasn't long before both of them were singing along with the radio while decorating the tree.

As she hauled decorations out of the box, she'd tell him a little story of where it came from. He was overly dramatic with his eye expressions making her laugh even more.

When she pulled a small red and white candy cane salt-dough ornament out of the box, she gasped. "Oh my God! I haven't seen this one in years. My grandmother and I made these as presents one year for everyone in the family...I was about ten. They all fell apart except this one." As a tear fell, she added, "I used clear nail polish on this one...which is why it's still here."

Leaning over, he took the ornament from her hand and studied it carefully. "This is something you should take home and share with your daughters."

Wiping the tear from her cheek, she whispered, "No, I don't think so. It belongs here…where Gram was. Who knows? Next year for Christmas, I might bring the girls here."

"You know, you can come back anytime you want to…the girls would have a lot of fun swimming in the lake like we used to do."

"Yeah, I know…I honestly don't know why I've stayed away so long….life, I guess." She didn't look him in the eye, afraid of what he would think. She knew she'd been weak, but didn't want him to see her that way.

"Okay, so change it. You've proved you can come up here and get work done. You've proved that you can keep a fire going. What more is there to do? Oh wait! You still have to learn to cook on a woodstove when the power goes out!" he teased.

Laughter mixed in with the threatened tears. Grabbing the ornament from him, she hung it on the tree and joked with him, "I don't know. You keep acting like that and there might not be any turkey for you. I'll feed your share to Minnie."

"You wouldn't dare?"

"Oh, don't push me, Mister. You'd be surprised at what I am capable of," she giggled.

More teasing followed and Jenny sang along with the radio with Matt humming beside her. When it was finally decorated, he turned on the battery operated lights. Blue, green, red, and white lights shone lightly through the branches and Jenny couldn't help it...she giggled.

"Don't laugh! The lights will be brighter by the time it gets dark outside. You wait and see!"

Laughing, she asked, "You want to go another round of Monopoly with me? I'm feeling like my luck has changed."

"Um, yeah, but I actually have to take a quick run back to my cabin real quick. I...uh...forgot something," he told her.

"You want company?"

He shook his head. "No, the snow is coming down harder. I'm probably going to have to get a little shoveling done and, when I get back, I want to get that tree outside here taken care of."

"No problem…I have plenty I should be doing," she replied quickly. "I…uh…have work."

"Well, don't work too hard. I plan on kicking your butt later in Monopoly and I don't want you to use the excuse that you're tired when you lose," he laughed.

Placing her hands on his upper arms, she turned him around and shoved him toward the door. "Just go…You want to leave…leave. I have work to do!" She plastered a smile on her face and watched him put on his coat.

"You sure you're not mad at me?" he asked.

"I'm not mad," she growled. "A little disappointed because I wanted another ride, but I do have things to do. I was doing great before you came…I think I can handle a few hours alone," she laughed.

After zipping up his coat, Matt reached out and pulled her into a bear hug. Stunned, Jenny could barely breathe. Her own arms went around his and she breathed in his outdoorsy scent.

It may have only lasted a few seconds, but she was breathless when he pulled away. But, he didn't go far and soon he had leaned down and touched his lips lightly to hers. She wasn't sure how long she stood there and when she finally let out a breath, she realized he had already gone out the door.

Chapter 10

Jenny leaned up against the door...her fingers touching her lips...the same ones that Matt had just kissed. That was something she hadn't expected...at all. Heck, she wasn't even prepared for the hug he'd bestowed on her let alone a kiss!

Well, it obviously cleared things up a little for her, though. Matt was interested in her. Was she interested in him? Then, she laughed. Really! How could she not be interested in him? He was good looking, funny, smart, caring...and then she realized. She'd already spent the last twenty-four hours being interested in him. Why was it such a surprise? Was it too soon?

Thinking about her predicament, she didn't know whether to laugh or cry. Her ex had gotten over her quickly. Why shouldn't she do the same? Then again, she had a problem with him bringing someone into the girl's lives so quickly after the divorce. But...she didn't have to have them meet him.

Tired of her brain zigzagging between thoughts, she finally let out a breath and laughed. Laughed because she was actually having fun and it was a pretty good feeling to know that someone thought she was interesting enough to want to spend time with her.

Standing up, she chided herself for such silly thoughts. She should just go with the flow...let what happens happen and not worry about every little thing.

Grabbing the bucket of water, rubber gloves, and a scrubber, she bent over and started cleaning the oven in the woodstove. Cleaning always took her mind of things and, before long she had it scrubbed clean and had only burned herself once.

Just as she finished, the power came back on and she squealed in delight waking up Minnie who was lying in the chair with Mickey. Minnie started bouncing around and barking while she laughed and let out a whoop of joy.

After all of the excitement, Minnie ran to the door and announced with a loud bark that she was ready to go outside. "Okay, Min. Give me a second to get dressed. It's brutal out there."

A half hour later and back in the cabin, Jenny was wondering what was taking Matt so long. She thought he'd be back by now and then scolded herself for wondering. He was a grown man and didn't owe her the time of day. And…when he came back, they'd have to talk about that kiss…she wasn't sure if she was ready.

Instead of letting her impatience get to her, she hauled out her grandmother's sewing machine out of the back room and the material that was secured inside a plastic tote to keep the mice out. It was all about making good use of her time.

It wasn't too long before she had finished a coat for Minnie and a flannel shirt, gloves, and a scarf for Matt that she heard the sound of the snow machine. Grabbing the items off the table, she quickly took them into her room and set them to the side to wrap later.

She stepped back into the kitchen just as Matt came through the door. After greeting Minnie, he turned and looked at her.

"Do I owe you an apology?" he asked, his eyes making direct contact with hers.

She wasn't sure how she did it, but she managed a smile. "No, you don't. We're adults. I think we can handle a kiss."

When he smiled at her, she felt the telltale heat rising and knew that her face must look flushed. She quickly told him, "Did you get everything done? Minnie and I just came inside a little while ago. It's so cold out there, why don't you forget about the trees today."

"Yeah, I was also gone much longer than I thought I would be. I grabbed the plow truck and cleared out my driveway. My father will show up sometime tomorrow night to get this done. If the truck won't do this drive, his bulldozer will."

"Your father has a bulldozer?" she laughed.

"Oh yes. A bulldozer, a dump truck, a backhoe…he's got them all. They're his toys," he laughed. "Well, he uses them for his work, but he still calls them his toys."

"Well, I bet they're a blast to drive around. I've always wanted to drive a bulldozer," she told him. "Even when I was little, I wanted cars and trucks. Never really played with dolls."

"Maybe we can let you try his out sometime, but for now, we should think about dinner. I grabbed a frozen pizza out of my freezer, but it's not your normal frozen pizza from the grocery store."

"Did you make them?" she asked.

"Hell no! I can make pizza, but nothing beats Pizza Hut. Every time I go near a Pizza Hut, I ask them to make up a couple without cooking them. Then, I throw them into the pizza oven on the back deck whenever I want. We can use the woodstove oven," he told her and then opened the oven door. "I see you even cleaned it up today."

"Well, I thought the turkey was going in there tomorrow and I'm a little partial to not

102

having it dusty," she snickered. "And, pizza sounds good."

Clearing his voice, he took her hand in his. "My parents both want you to come to Christmas dinner tomorrow."

She felt the heat of his hand in hers and it was as if her heart skipped a beat. "Um…then who will cook your dinner?" she joked. Anything to get her mind off the fact that this man was sending off electric jolts with his touch.

"Oh, you are a funny one, Jenny. However, my parents would love it if you would come. My sister will be there with my nieces and her husband. My Aunt Jane and Uncle Bud will be there, too, and I am assuming a few cousins or stragglers. There are usually about fifteen to twenty of us each year for Christmas dinner."

Wow…she hadn't had a Christmas dinner with that many people since she was a kid. For some reason, after she became an adult things changed. "You sure they wouldn't mind? I don't want to impose on them."

Letting go of his hand, he stood back and laughed. "You obviously don't know my parents well. Their house is open to anyone who needs anything. Growing up, we always had company and someone staying with us for days at a time. My parent's house has always been crowded, which is just the way they like it."

Jenny couldn't imagine what that was like growing up. Being an only child, she loved it when family came to stay. Other than that, it had only been she and her parents.

Nodding her head, she looked at him and said, "I'm game if you are, but I have to bring something. You want to help me make cookies?"

"I would love to, but first things first. It's Christmas Eve and one of my family's traditions has been making hot chocolate, building a bonfire, and watching the stars. You up for that? If you are, I'm going to clear a spot for the bonfire later."

Jenny thought it sounded wonderful. "I am. I will get the cookies started and you can join in when you come in."

Turning on the radio, Jenny hummed along with the music while she made cookies. This was certainly not how she had expected to spend her Christmas. Who would have thought that she would one day be spending Christmas with her girlhood crush? Having dinner with his family?

As she put a sheet full of sugar cookies into the oven, she set the timer and looked outside. Matt was throwing snowballs up into the air and Minnie was doing her best to catch them all. Turning around, she glanced at Mickey who was still lying in the chair. When he caught her looking, he let out a meow, as if to say he was just fine.

Noticing that Matt had left his phone on the table, she glanced at the clock thinking it might be a good time to try the girls again. With three bars, she was pretty sure she could get through and dialed. After the fourth ring, it went to voice mail.

"Hi! It's me. Just hoped to speak to the girls. I'll try them tomorrow."

Shaking her head, she couldn't imagine why Kevin wasn't answering his cell phone. He lived on it and had no problem answering calls no matter where he was or who he was with.

Chapter 11

The wind blew around them and gentle flakes fell from the night sky, but Jenny didn't feel cold. Sitting on logs that Matt had pulled out of the shed they held mugs of hot coffee and enjoyed the heat from the fire.

"This is amazing," Jenny whispered. "Thank you."

Matt turned and smiled. "It's nice just to sit back and enjoy nature, even when it's brutal. This place is inundated with people all summer long, but very few come to enjoy it in the winter."

"They don't know what they're missing."

Reaching over, he rested his hand on her knee. "No, they don't."

Even through the snow pants she wore, she could feel his touch on her skin and inside she melted. Was it just the fact that she'd had a crush on him so many years ago? Was it just the fact that she had been without a man in her life for so long?

While she tried coming up with an answer, Matt leaned over and told her, "If you keep looking like that, I might just have to kiss you again."

Eyes wide and holding her breath, she glanced his way to see him with a grin on his face. "Um…I…"

"Does it bother you that I said that?"

"No…it's just…"

"I really would like to kiss you again," he said with a more serious tone.

Bringing up the mug of hot chocolate to her lips, she took a sip and swallowed, never taking her eyes off him. She was shocked…well, not as much shocked as she was anxious. Why did he have to talk about it. Why didn't he just kiss her?

As if he had read her mind, Matt reached over and took the mug out of her hands and placed it beside his on the small log in front of them. Pulling his log closer to hers, he then leaned forward. She could see the sparkle in his eyes and the seriousness of his expression.

She wasn't sure if she leaned forward to meet him or he had come forward the rest of the way, but suddenly his lips were on hers. His lips were firm, but soft and obviously knew what they were doing. The warmth spread throughout her body and she started to panic.

Pulling away from the kiss, she rested a hand on his chest. "Matt," she whispered, "I don't know if I am ready for this."

Matt leaned his forehead against hers and looked her in the eye. "I don't know if I am either, but I'm ready to take a chance."

Placing her hands on his shoulders, she whispered, "I just...I don't know if I am ready."

Matt lifted his head and looked directly into her eyes. "It's okay. I've been there. However, I will tell you this. I don't give up that easily. I think we have something...I guess I just want to explore it to see what it is."

Explore it? Was she ready to take a chance again? Risk getting hurt again? She wanted to, but she didn't know if she could.

Matt took all seriousness out of the conversation and laughed. "You don't have to say anything. Let's not rush it…let's just spend the rest of our time together getting to know each other without any expectations."

Keeping her eyes on his, she asked, "Are you sure? You probably think I'm a nut job. Heck, sometimes I think I'm a nut job."

Matt pulled her closer to him and wrapped his arms around her. Why was he being so nice to her? She so badly wanted to explore this thing with him, but could she do it without getting hurt? Or hurting him?

She knew Matt had been hurt when he got divorced. He hadn't said too much about it, but she knew what that meant. In her experience, men who didn't talk about it were the ones who hurt the most.

When Matt stepped back from her, he told her, "I'm sorry if I made you uncomfortable, but I've learned one thing in life. If you want something, you have to go for it. Now, let's forget all about this and get inside. The fire is dying down and it is getting colder."

Leaning down, he picked up the coffee mugs and motioned her to lead the way.

The first thing Matt did when he came inside was to grab his phone, which had a blinking red light. "Hmm...Excuse me a second while I listen to this voice mail. Give me just a second and I'll help you get the fire stoked."

Jenny had just grabbed a log to put on the fire, when he stated, "Jenny, it was for you. Kevin. He wants you to call him immediately."

Dropping the log, Jenny ran to the phone. Why would Kevin call her back? Something must be wrong.

Her hands shaking, she dialed the phone. Kevin answered on the first ring.

"Where have you been? I've been trying to reach you for over an hour."

"We...I was just outside. What's going on?" she demanded.

"It's Mia. The girl is acting up and I'm not going to put up with it anymore."

"What do you mean? What's happened?"

Kevin started talking so fast she had to tell him to repeat everything again, but slower.

"Mia is being a brat. I'm assuming you told her to not like Melanie? Well, believe me, that was a big mistake."

Gasping, she yelled, "I didn't say anything of the sort. In fact, I told them they had to respect her. What exactly is Mia doing?"

Kevin's voice rose. "Mia told Melanie that you and I were getting back together and she should just leave."

"She said that? Really?" Jenny was shocked. She had never heard Mia even say anything close to that and thought Mia understood that they were divorced.

"She did. Then, she went on to tell Melanie that you were prettier than she was and that I still loved you."

"What? Seriously? She said that?" Poor Mia. She obviously was upset. Now, if she could just tell Kevin how to handle it.

"Yes, she said that and now she's in her room on Christmas Eve!" he muttered.

"Kevin, would you let me talk to her? This isn't unusual…or at least I don't think it is. Just don't yell at her. Ask her what is bothering her. Talk to her."

"You can talk to her, but she better understand that this type of behavior is unacceptable. Poor Melanie has been crying her eyes out since they got back."

"Well, you can be concerned about Melanie, but please put Mia on the phone."

Glancing over at Matt, she whispered, "I'm sorry."

He walked up to her and patted her on the back. "No problem. Take all the time you need. I'm going to take Minnie out to give you some privacy."

She watched him put on his coat and gloves. Who was this man? He was calm...considerate...sweet. Why wasn't she ready to jump?

"Mom?" Mia's voice quavered.

"Oh, Sweetie! What happened?"

"Mom, she's terrible. All she wanted to do was buy stuff for herself when we were shopping. With Daddy's credit card!" she cried.

"Mia, that's not up to you to say anything about."

"But I remember Daddy yelling at you all the time about money. He's just going to yell at her. Then, she got mean. Said I needed to stop acting bratty and that I was just a kid and would figure it out when I got older."

"Mia, can I ask you a question?"

"Yes, but I don't want to be in trouble. Daddy yelled at me and told me I have to stay in my room," she sniveled.

"Oh, Mia. Did you tell Melanie that Daddy still loves me?"

Silence loomed on the other end of the phone. "Mia?"

"Yes. I said it, but only because I was mad at her."

Trying to keep the laughter out of her voice, she said calmly, "You need to apologize. Those words are unacceptable and you know it. You don't say things to hurt people, even if they hurt you first."

"Can you come get me? I don't want to be here. I will say I'm sorry, but I want to leave."

Jenny felt the tears well up in her eyes. "Honey, I'm snowed in at the moment. We've had a lot of snow and ice. We will have the best Christmas when you come home. I promise."

"Okay, but I miss you, Mama. I don't like this," Mia cried. "I think Andi wants to talk to you, too."

After reassuring Mia that they would see each other in a week and talking to Andi, who seemed to have no problems at all with the situation, she hung up the phone.

She only hoped that she had handled the situation with Mia well enough to help her get through the next few days. From what Mia had said, she was actually trying to protect Melanie...not hurt her...and Melanie had overreacted.

Realizing that Matt was still outside, Jenny went to the window and looked outside just as he was coming up the steps. He gave her the biggest smile before he went to the door. Yes, there was something definitely there between them.

Chapter 12

"Is everything okay?" Matt asked as he came through the door.

"Yeah, it is, but my oldest is having a hard time…wanted me to come get her," she answered. "First time she has met her father's girlfriend and I don't think it's going well."

"That's got to be tough. Did you want to go to her? I can take you in my truck from my place," Matt offered.

Again, Matt was proving that he wasn't the average man…at least in her eyes. No man that she ever knew probably would have offered to take her home on icy roads just to see her daughter, even if it was Christmas Eve.

"Thanks, but no…she understands about the storm…I talked to her. Kevin's girlfriend did something to upset her and she said some things she shouldn't have."

"Poor kid. That age is a difficult one."

"Yeah, it doesn't help that her father's girlfriend is so young, either. I'm sure that this thing is harder on her than I realize...her sister, too."

His hand reached out and lifted her chin up so that she was looking at him. Her skin tingled where he touched.

"Is this why you are hesitant to see where this thing between us goes?" he murmured.

She could only whisper, "Yes."

Leaning down to her, he touched his lips to her forehead and then stood back. "You have a lot on your plate and that I understand. Don't stress about it."

Stepping back, he clapped his hands. "Okay. The cookies are done. It's time for pizza and...some music. Get that radio cranking!"

Giggling, Jenny turned on the radio and turned it up every time Matt yelled, "Louder!" Minnie sat on the floor wagging her tail while Mickey looked at them like they were all crazy.

When Rocking Around the Christmas Tree came on the radio, he gave her one look that had her laughing harder than she ever had. His index finger crookedly motioned her to come closer and all she could do was laugh. Still evading him, she skipped around to the kitchen table until he caught her by her waist and took her hand in his. Before long, he was twirling her around the kitchen while they laughed.

Before long, however, Jenny danced her way over to the table and sat down. "You know, I'm not as young as I used to be. I need to sit."

"Oh, come on! You know, I think you're just afraid that my dancing skills are going to show you up!" he smiled.

"You probably can. I haven't been dancing in years."

Jenny watched as he moved to the music while he checked on the pizza. She loved that he made her laugh, even when she felt like she was on the verge of a crying fit. She'd had plenty of those in the last six months, but after this week, she doubted that there would be many more. Life was suddenly looking pretty good.

The pizza was amazing. She had eaten at Pizza Hut many times and it was one of the best, but this one tasted better. Perhaps it was the woodstove. Perhaps it was the company.

As she took the last bite of a slice, he asked, "More?"

"God no! I am stuffed. You have the last piece. I can't eat it."

"Well, if you can't, I will," he chuckled lightly. "I have to say that this is my favorite pizza ever. Maybe it's the company," he added with a wink."

"Yeah, well, like I said, I couldn't eat another bite. I can't believe I ate that much and now I'm supposed to eat a big dinner at your parent's?"

"You don't have to if you don't want to. We actually don't sit down to a formal dinner. It's more of a buffet style dinner and you sit where you can fit," he told her. "Honestly, you'll feel right at home."

Jenny cleaned up the dishes in the kitchen and then glanced at the clock. It was only nine, but it felt so much later.

"I…uh…I think I'm going to turn in. I'm exhausted," she told him. "Is this too early for you?"

Shaking his head, he pulled off his fleece jacket and folded it onto the back of the chair. "No, go ahead if you want. If you don't mind, I'll probably sit for a little while and then take Minnie out one more time for before I turn in."

"Oh, I didn't think of that. It's been a long time since I've had a dog," she told him. "Kevin isn't exactly an animal person…wasn't a fan of cats let alone a dog."

"In my case, the saying that dog is a man's best friend has rang true. I've never been without one…can't imagine not having a buddy to hang out with."

Jenny thought about this for a moment and said, "Will you help me find one? A dog would make the perfect gift for the girls when they get back."

She watched as his eyes lit up. "What kind of dog? A puppy? Big? Small?"

"I don't know. I haven't thought that far ahead," she admitted.

Sitting down beside him at the table, he filled her in on the many different types of dogs he'd had as a boy growing up and which types he thought would be a good fit for Mia and Andi.

She told him of the little Toy Fox Terrier she'd had as a child and, after it died, how she'd never wanted another.

"You have a big heart, Jenny. You need to share it. Look at your cat. Now, I've never understood cats, but the one you have is almost human," he smiled.

"I brought Mickey home and Kevin wasn't a fan. He's been by my side for the last fifteen years and, a lot of the time, he's been my sounding board." Laughing, she questioned, "Does that make me the crazy cat lady?"

"If talking to your animal makes you a crazy person, then I guess I'm one, too because I talk to Minnie all the time. You'd think she'd get sick of me, but so far so good."

"Can't imagine it. She worships you. Do you know of any breeders up this way that might have any puppies?"

"I can make a few calls. When were you planning on heading back? Where exactly is it that you live?" he inquired.

"Gorham. The girls won't be back until the first of the New Year, but I wanted to be home a few days early to get Christmas ready for them."

Leaning over, he looked at her closely. "I have an aunt down in Buxton. It's a beautiful area. If you want, I can make a call the day after Christmas. You sure you want a puppy?"

"Yes, I'm sure. I think it would take the girls' minds off all this crazy stuff for a bit."

"It will. That I can guarantee," he said as he got up from the table. "Now, you said over an hour and a half ago that you wanted to go to bed. Tomorrow is Christmas. I wonder if Santa will come tonight?" he questioned with a sparkle in his eye.

Jenny lay in bed for an hour before she could hear the subtle snore of Matt out in the main room. Sneaking out of her bed, she carefully picked up the presents she had made for him and the one for Minnie and put them under the tree. While she had wished she could do more, she hadn't exactly counted on meeting him again.

She often wondered what had happened to him. Her girlhood crush had seemed silly once she'd become an adult, but meeting him again...she couldn't describe it. He was everything he was as a teenager and more. Still kind...still funny...still attractive.

What was she going to do about him? She'd told him she wasn't ready and the truth was that she was scared. She didn't want to do anything that could harm the girls, but it was more than that. How could she know that things would work out?

One of the first problems was that they lived so far away. Matt had lived here all his life. There was no way that he would move and she shouldn't expect him to. She couldn't move her girls out of their school and away from their friends. It wouldn't be fair to them. So how could it work? It wouldn't, so it was probably better to just keep things friendly between them without getting involved...no matter how difficult it was.

Chapter 13

Jenny stretched and opened her eyes. The coffee pot gurgled out in the main room and she looked at the clock beside her. Almost eight and she felt like she could've slept for another eight. She'd had trouble sleeping and she blamed it on the man that had started the coffee.

The truth was that all she could think about was the fact that she had power back, the danger of falling trees was over, and he'd still spent the night. It had seemed natural. Neither one had mentioned that he should have gone back to his own house. The truth was she hadn't wanted him to.

Rolling over, she grabbed her robe from the side of the bed and slowly put her arms in it and crawled out of bed. Glancing in the mirror, she nearly laughed out loud. All of the tossing and turning had not done her hair any wonders. It didn't help that all she could do was wash it in the sink. Grabbing a brush, she managed to pull it back into a ponytail and hope for the best.

Walking into the main room, she was surprised to find it empty apart from Mickey who was eating his breakfast in front of the stove. Leaning down, she stroked his fur. "Merry Christmas, Mickey!"

Going to the door, she looked outside, but there was no sign of Matt or Minnie. Turning to the coffee pot, which had stopped gurgling, she noticed a note on the counter sticking to her coffee mug.

"Be back in about an hour," it stated. What a great way to start Christmas and then it dawned on her that if he hadn't been there, she would have woken up alone anyway. Pouring herself a cup, she glanced down at the tree and noticed two gifts underneath that hadn't been there last night. Laughing, she went over to the tree.

She looked at the largest, which had her name on it and then the other held Mickey's. The gifts she had put under the tree last night were still there.

After finishing her coffee quickly, Jenny got dressed. It was snowing heavy and she'd love to get some pictures of the cabin for the girls.

She knew they probably wouldn't make it to the camp until the weather warmed, but wanted them to see it like this.

A few minutes later, she was outdoors, camera in hand and snapping pictures of the cabin. Deciding that she wanted to get pictures of the trees that had fallen, she wandered to the side of the camp, snapping pictures that would keep the memories alive of standing in Matt's arms. After all, she would be leaving soon and it could be a long time before she saw him again.

Wandering around the camp, she noticed that the tracks where the snowmobile were had been covered up in snow already. The snow pelted her face, but having too much fun, she barely noticed it. She did see some other tracks on the snow covered lake and it almost looked like a cat track.

Following the tracks over the snow, she had hopes of getting a picture of it in the distance. She wasn't stupid enough to get that close, but figured it was probably a bobcat. The tracks were big, but not big enough to be a mountain lion. Of course, mountain lions in Maine were rare, but she had heard of sightings.

As she followed them, her mind drifted to what would await her back at the cabin. She imagined that she and Matt would exchange gifts, eat a small breakfast, and then get ready to go to his parent's for an early dinner. Just maybe he would try to kiss her again. The thought made her laugh. Could she be any more contradictory?

Yes, she wanted him, but she had no clue how to make it work. The girls were another hurdle that she wasn't sure she could get over. These things could either drive them apart or pull them together.

Glancing down at the tracks in front of her, she realized that she had traveled to the end of the cove and glanced back toward the cabin. The snow was falling hard enough that she couldn't see it anymore. The tracks went into the woods and she figured just a little farther wouldn't hurt.

Inside the woods, she snapped pictures of the snow on the trees, icicles hanging off branches, and more pictures of the tracks that had called to her to get out and enjoy it all. It wasn't until she had followed them further into the woods that she realized the snow was coming down faster now.

Turning around, she started to follow her tracks back, but after a few feet realized they were covered in snow. Doing her best to make out the indentations she kept going until she couldn't see them anymore at all. Gasping, she realized she was lost. She hadn't thought that she'd gone that far into the woods. She should have reached the open lake by now.

Stuffing the camera inside her jacket, she shook the snow off her and looked around. Did the tracks go in a straight line or had they veered to the left? Or was it right? Trying to think which direction she'd travelled left her feeling bewildered. She would not panic. She'd grown up here and knew these woods like the back of her hand.

Still, the woods had changed immensely over the years and it had been about twenty years or more since she'd been in them. She tried to think about the distance she'd walked and in which direction the tracks had led.

If the sun had been out, none of this would have been a problem, as she could have figured out what direction she needed to go in. But then again, if the sun were out she would be able to see more than two feet in front of her.

Finding a snow covered log, she swiped at the snow and sat down. No need to use more energy than she had to. She could at least sit for a minute to try to get her bearings.

She thought back to what she had learned about survival when she was younger. For many years, her grandfather had taught and questioned her on what to do if you were lost in the woods, stranded in a boat, or even attacked by a bear. Living up here in the northern woods of Maine, your life could depend on it.

Almost as if a lightbulb had gone off in her head, Jenny jumped up. Moss! She remembered what her grandfather had taught her when she was about seven. "North. When you here, remember it's north. We live in the north woods on the north side of the lake and, don't forget, moss grows on the north side of the tree."

How could she have forgotten that? Now, if she could just find a tree with moss on it she would be doing well. Laughing, she ran off to inspect the trees and was elated when she came across an old oak tree that had moss growing on one side. Well, that answered that question. Now, if she could just find the lake and the camp.

Trudging through the snow, her hands had begun to feel numb and she realized that the gloves she wore were just not insulated enough for this kind of weather. Her feet were good and her face was covered with her scarf, but her hands were showing signs of frostbite. Unzipping the pockets of her coat, she stuck them inside and hoped for the best.

Arriving at what she knew was the edge of the lake, she almost screamed with joy. In the distance, she could hear a snowmobile and she wondered if it was Matt on his way back from his house. He probably didn't even realize she was missing yet and she'd really like to keep it from him. He'd probably tell her she was stupid for following the tracks and scold her.

No, he wouldn't. That would be something that Kevin would do, not Matt. Matt would be happy that she was able to find her way home and leave it at that.

As she started across the lake, the snow started to let up a little. The muscles in her legs had started to burn. She knew she was a little out of shape, but this much? Her breathing was getting heavier, but she didn't want to slow down. If that was Matt on the snowmobile earlier, she didn't want him to worry when he got to camp and realized she wasn't there. She hadn't even left him a note!

Hurrying her steps even more, she was aware of every muscle in her body by now. Her arms ached, her back hurt, and her knees throbbed. If there was anything left of her by the time she got back to camp, she'd be shocked.

Minutes later, she heard the sound of the snowmobile off in the distance again. The snow had almost stopped by now and she was able to make out the other side of the cove. She was at least a mile off course and she wanted to cry. With the snow at least two feet deep, walking in it wasn't easy, but she wasn't about to give in to the tears that threatened.

Just ahead of her was the old red barn where all the teenagers hung out. It wasn't really a barn, but that's what everyone called it around here. A big red building where you could dock your boat, fill up on gas, and get something to eat. As a teenager, she'd even worked there one summer.

Now, looking at it, she only wanted to jump up and down and throw a hissy fit. It wouldn't do her any good, but it would beat walking the mile or more back to camp.

Stopping in the middle of the deep snow, she heard the sound of the snowmobile getting closer. Maybe, just maybe, she could convince the rider to give her a quick ride back to her camp.

When she saw the snowmobile come into view, though, her heart gave a lurch. It was Matt. Was she right in guessing that he wouldn't be mad? There was only one way to tell and she tried to stand taller in the snow and waved her hands in the air to get his attention.

Chapter 14

She heard him yelling before he even shut the snowmobile down. "Jenny! What are you doing?"

"I...uh...just took a walk to take some pictures. I didn't realize how far I wandered," she told him. "I'm so glad to see you, though. I forgot how out of shape I am,"

"I cannot tell you how worried I've been. I got back to the camp and, when I realized you weren't there, well...I thought the worst."

Seeing the worry in his eyes, Jenny felt horrible. "I'm so sorry, Matt. I just went out to get pictures and well...I sort of got lost."

"Lost? Jenny, are you okay?" he asked as he got off the snowmobile.

"Um, yeah...my hands are little cold, but other than that I'm good."

When he reached down and picked her up, Jenny let out a yelp.

"What are you doing? I can walk!"

"I know, but let's get you home quickly and get you warmed up." He then set her down on the back of the snowmobile and climbed on the front. Turning around, he asked one more time. "Are you okay?"

Jenny could only nod her head. She'd never felt worse in her life, but it didn't have anything to do with her hands, the cold, or the snow that had started falling again. She was disappointed for having made him worry. He wasn't angry at all, which very ironically, made her feel a lot worse.

Back at the camp, he pulled the snowmobile as close as he could get and quickly shut off the engine. She stood up and was swept again into his arms.

"I can walk!" she told him.

"No, let's get you inside quick to get you warmed up."

Inside, he set her down in front of the woodstove and helped her peel off her jacket, scarf, and her mittens. Her hands were red and still tingling and she placed them close to the stove.

"No, not too close," he murmured. "You don't want to damage them more. You have to warm them slowly."

Pulling her hands back, she looked at him closely and saw the worry lines on his forehead and a frown instead of his normal smile.

"I'm sorry for worrying you. It was stupid," she whispered.

"No, it's okay. I'm just glad you're okay. How are your feet?"

She wiggled her toes. "Fine. I was just starting to feel cold when you showed up to rescue me."

He pulled the rocking chair a little closer to the stove and guided her to sit down. He then pulled her boots off and her thick, wool socks. After a careful inspection of her feet, he told her, "Put them by the stove, but not too close."

She watched as he moved around the camp with ease. He turned off the coffee pot after pouring two cups and added one sugar and cream to hers. Handing it to her, he asked, "You sure you'll be okay to go to my parents?"

She laughed. She couldn't help it. It just felt nice to have someone worry about her needs. Usually, she was too busy worrying about someone else's.

"I'm fine. I can't wait. What time do you want to be there?"

"Anytime we get there is fine," he smiled. Then he winked. "Now, sit right there. I believe Santa came to visit last night!"

Laughing, she pulled the throw that he dropped in her lap over her legs. She watched as he carefully picked up one of the presents under the tree.

"Oh look! This one is for Mickey. Mickey, you want to come open your present with you Mama?" he asked while reaching down to pick him up.

As he put him down on her lap, he laughed, "Well, after picking him up, I don't think he probably needs what Santa left him."

Giggling, Jenny rubbed the back of Mickey's neck and told him, "Don't you listen to him, Mickey. If Santa thought you needed to lose weight, he wouldn't have given you treats."

At the word treat, Mickey meowed, sending both she and Matt into a fit of giggles. Opening the package, she quickly opened the container of treats and gave one to the purring cat who promptly grabbed it and jumped out of her lap to run into the bedroom.

"Can you grab that one under there for Minnie?"

Minnie, hearing her name, walked over and rested her head in Jenny's lap. Matt brought the package over and leaned down to Minnie.

"Get it, Minnie! Open it up!" Minnie took the end of the package in her mouth and carefully pulled until the paper started to tear.

"Oh my God! How did you teach her that?" Jenny laughed.

"Minnie is very teachable," he answered. "And she's a sweetheart. Aren't you, Minnie?"

After receiving a bark in return, Matt opened up the rest of the package to discover a bright pink dog coat with white stripes. He held it up in awe. "Did you make this?

"Yeah, another one of the things my grandmother taught me. Her old sewing machine is here, along with a few tubs of fabric, so I just threw it together the other day."

After calling Minnie over, he put it on her and inspected it. "Well, it certainly is going to make a statement. Minnie is going to be the best dressed dog around here!"

"Matt, go get the other one under the tree. It has your name on it." Jenny couldn't wait to see his face when he opened it.

When Matt came back to her from the tree, he carried two presents. One he handed to her. "This is from me."

"You didn't have to get me anything. But, I'm glad you did. I love Christmas," she laughed.

"I can see that," he chuckled.

Both Matt and Jenny concentrated on unwrapping their presents. Both were careful not to rip the paper until their eyes met. As if on cue, they both laughed and tore into them, laughter filling the cabin as they did.

Jenny's wrapping paper came off to reveal bubble wrap. Carefully, unrolling it, she gasped when she saw what was inside.

The miniature wooden sculpture was the perfect rendition of Mickey. Every detail, from the shape of his eyes to the very tip of his tail, was perfect. Tears filled her eyes.

By this time, Matt had unwrapped his package. Inside was a blue and white flannel shirt she had sewn, a scarf, and a pair of flannel lined gloves she had made from the left overs.

Matt didn't say a word. Just stood up, set his presents on the table and then leaned over her. "Merry Christmas, Jenny."

Before his lips met hers, Jenny whispered, "Merry Christmas."

Chapter 15

Jenny set her glass down on the table. Looking around the room, she smiled at the odd array of people that sat at the table and milled about the house. Matt had tried to describe to her what it would be like, but she had thought he was exaggerating. She was pleasantly surprised to find that he had not.

Matt's parents were the down-to-earth kind of people that everyone liked. His mother had been a school teacher and knew everyone in the area. His father was a caretaker for many of the properties on the lake, but used his skills to do many other jobs for the locals.

An elderly neighbor, one that Matt had described as a Nosey Nellie, sat across from Jenny and was extremely inquisitive about her life in Gorham. Jenny answered every one of her questions with a smile.

His nieces, too, were just like he described. Bubbly, talkative, and loud. They reminded her of Mia and Andi. One second best friends...the next second fighting.

Matt seemed to fit right in with everyone in the room. She watched as he laughed with an older gentlemen standing at the kitchen counter and then with a boy in his teens. He knew everyone and she could tell he liked them all.

This would not be Kevin's type of Christmas. Kevin was all about showing off what he had. Christmas dinners were all a formal affair and everyone had to be on their best behavior.

What had she seen in him? It was strange to think about now. When she had met him, he seemed to have it all and, what he didn't have, he had a goal to get.

It was funny how she'd once thought that she wanted all of the things he wanted. She wasn't exactly sure when she'd changed, but she should have seen the divorce coming a long time before it actually happened.

Last Christmas had been a disaster. He'd invited all these people from his work and actually requested that she uninvited some of her friends that he didn't think measured up to his standards. Needless to say, things did not go smoothly.

This year was something else entirely and she knew she could actually put this one in the books for one the best Christmas' as an adult. The only thing missing were her children.

Matt walked over to the table and sat in the chair next to her. He asked, "You doing okay over here?"

"I am. Thank you for bringing me. It's been a lot of fun," she smiled.

He leaned in closer and whispered, "I have one more present for you, but it's not ready yet. You got about ten minutes."

Laughing, she pushed him away. "Another present? You didn't have to do that. Just being here is present enough. Your family is wonderful."

At that moment, his Aunt Tilly stepped into the room. When she spotted Matt and Jenny, she took a few steps forward and then pointed. "You didn't tell me you finally found a woman who would put up with you?"

Jenny looked at Matt with question in her eyes. She had just met his Aunt Tilly not an hour before and had answered question after question about their relationship.

"Aunt Tilly, I'm sorry. Let me introduce you to Jenny. She's been coming to Moosehead since she was a young girl."

Matt whispered into her ear, "Alzheimer's...beginning stages, so we just go along with it."

Standing up, Jenny walked over to his Aunt Tilly and introduced herself. She then answered many of the same questions she'd been asked before. When the little woman suddenly turned around and walked off, Matt smiled and grabbed Jenny's hand.

"Thanks. Now it is time for your other present. Follow me!" he told her and went toward the back of the house.

After going up a set of stairs, Matt led Jenny into a room that was obviously being used as a sewing room. However, in the middle of the table sat a laptop. When he directed her to sit down, she was confused.

What was Matt doing? Did he find her a puppy and wanted to show her pictures? Excitement filled her, but when he leaned over her back and brought up Skype, she was even more confused. What was going on?

When Mia and Andi's faces popped up on Skype, Jenny squealed with delight. "What are you guys doing? Oh, look at you two!"

"Daddy said we could Skype with you. I miss you, Mommy!" Andi wiped her eyes and Jenny soothed her.

"It's okay, Baby. Mommy's going to be back in a few days to get our Christmas ready and then you'll be back home. Are you having fun with Daddy?"

Mia spoke up and listed off about a hundred items that Santa had left for her and her sister. Andi sat there with a half-smile, not knowing whether to be happy or sad.

After another minute or two, Kevin was behind the screen telling the girls it was time to say goodbye. "Thank you, Kevin. Girls, I will see you soon. I love you!"

When the screen disappeared and her girls were no longer there for her to see, Jenny turned around to Matt only to discover he had left the room, giving her privacy.

Sitting there, she wondered how this whole thing had come about. When Kevin had told her he was taking the girls, he didn't even want her to call them every day. It was a chore just to get him to agree to a call on Christmas.

Matt stuck his head in the door with a big grin on her face. Jenny stood and tried to stop the tears from falling. Two steps later, she was in his arms, her arms wrapped around his neck.

Whispering, "How? I mean…why…how did you set this up?"

Laughing, Matt stepped back, his hands on her forearms. "Well, let me tell you something, it was no easy feat! Your ex-husband isn't exactly a friendly guy is he?"

"That would be one way to describe him," she laughed and cried at the same time. "How did this happen?"

Matt guided her back to the chair and sat down on a stepstool in front of it.

"This is what I did this morning. I grabbed my computer and brought it over here. Then I called him to set it up. He wasn't going to go for it, but...I can be pretty charming when I need to be," he grinned.

"Um, yeah, I know that," she admitted. "Was he awful to you?"

Matt shook his head. "Nope. I didn't give him a chance to be. Told him that this is what was going to happen and that if he didn't let you Skype with the girls, then next year, he wouldn't be able to Skype with them. It was a win-win situation for everyone. I hope you're not mad."

"Mad? How could I be mad?" Jenny giggled. "This was the absolute best present I ever could have gotten. I didn't expect to even be able to talk to them today and now...you did this!"

Wrapping her arms around him, Jenny leaned in and kissed his cheek. He smelled of wood smoke, pine needles, and Ivory soap. She'd never smelled anything better in her entire life.

Matt turned his head and claimed her lips. The kiss was sweet...it was promising...and everything she'd ever dreamed of, but...he ended it too quickly.

"I'm sorry, but if I don't stop, we're going to be in trouble," he stated. "And, when I say trouble, I mean having someone and catch us and then everyone in this house knows about it."

Standing up, she squeezed his arm. "Thank you again, Matt."

"No problem," he told her. "Now, let's go join the party."

When dark fell, someone suggested a bonfire and soon almost everyone was outside standing around a fire, drinking either from a bottle of wine, champagne, or a beer. Jenny had chosen wine. She'd never really been a beer drinker and hated the taste of champagne.

Matt stood behind her, one arm resting on her shoulder, trying to block the wind. When someone brought out marshmallows, it was a free for all to get one. Matt left her side for just a moment and came back holding onto two.

"Can I interest you in a toast?" he laughed.

"Absolutely!"

Jenny had not had this much fun in a long time. Here, she could be herself without worrying that someone was going to start judging her on whether she said the right thing, drank the wrong drink, or did something silly.

Matt had gone way out of his way to make her feel like she was part of the family. On top of that, he had made it possible for her to see her girls on Christmas Day. The only thing better would have been to see them in person.

The only bad thing was that she realized she was going back in a few days. This was something she didn't know how she was going to handle. Everything Matt did made her fall just a little bit more.

Chapter 16

After having spent the next two days with Matt, Jenny fought the tears as she packed her Explorer. She didn't want to leave, but her life down south demanded her return. The girls...her work...all of it demanded that she be there.

On Christmas night when they had returned to the camp, Matt and she had stayed up until three in the morning. They talked about the past and the summers they'd spent together as kids. He wasn't even surprised to find out that she'd finally parted ways with Sherri.

He had been surprised to find out that it hadn't happened sooner. "You deserve a better friend than that...I always thought so. I think everyone wondered why you brought Sherri here to the lake with you and your family. She was always so...negative," he told her.

Even that night, she'd stuck up for Sherri. "Yeah, but she had a rather rough life. I think she only did it to make her feel better about herself. It's sad, but true."

"Do you miss her?" he'd asked.

"I miss the idea of having a close friend," she'd answered.

She then went on to tell him how she'd lost many friends over the span of her marriage. None of them had met the standards that Kevin had placed and it was easier to remove friends from her life than to listen to Kevin talk bad about them.

When the subject of the future had come up, Matt had been very outspoken. "I want to see you again. Just because we live four hours away doesn't mean we're off limits."

"I know. It's just I know you're busy with your work and I don't want to be a distraction for you."

"You are going to be a distraction to me no matter where you are. Hell, you could move here fulltime and I'd still be distracted. How could a man not be?" he'd laughed.

Then he had turned the music on and they'd danced to several songs, before she had made an excuse. The truth was she hadn't trusted herself in Matt's arms.

As she placed a box of stuff into the back of her vehicle, she stopped and took a good look around. The snow was piled high and the lake was frozen. This, of course, was just a small part of the lake. Moosehead stretched out to almost a hundred and twenty square miles and she'd love to have time to go exploring further with Matt.

Yesterday, they'd gone out for a ride and travelled around the lake, but hadn't gone as far as she'd wanted to. When she was younger, she and her father had driven the snowmobiles down to Greenville. After exploring Sugar Island, they'd gone into town and ate at a little restaurant called Roadkill Café. She wasn't sure if it was still there and thought about stopping in on the way back.

Time had a way of getting away from you when you stayed at the lake and this trip had been no different. It seemed like she'd just arrived and staring at the camp, she wasn't ready to leave just yet.

Matt had taken a run over to his camp just an hour ago, saying that he had to get something. She'd hurried in packing the Explorer up, knowing it would be harder for her if they did that together.

She wondered if it were possible to fall in love with someone this quickly. Could it be love that she really felt for him? She wanted to believe it, but had trouble trusting her own instincts. She worried that she was simply jumping the gun at the first person that showed interest.

The sound of the snowmobile in the distance sent Jenny scrambling. Throwing the last box into the back, she shut the door and quickly went into the camp.

The outhouse was done…Matt had taken care of that when she'd turned her back on him for a minute. The fridge had been cleaned out and the garbage was now double-bagged and in her Explorer. A quick inspection and she couldn't think of anything else that needed to be done.

Except...saying goodbye to Matt. How she could do this without tears was beyond her...in less than a week, he'd given her hope that there wasn't anything wrong with he. That she could be in a successful relationship. The confidence to believe in herself and trust her own decisions. The belief that she was attractive. All of these things and more.

Saying goodbye now, after spending just a few days together? How was she going to do it?

She heard the sound of the snowmobile pulling up to the front and took a deep breath. An elephant stood on her chest making it almost impossible to do. Her hands shook and her eyes burned.

Matt walked in, took one look at her, and whispered, "Oh Jenny!" His arms held out wide, she quickly ran into them.

"I'm not ready to leave," she cried.

"I know, but just think. We have the Internet. We have the phone. Something our elders never had," he laughed.

"I know. Am I being foolish?"

Leaning down, he kissed the top of her head and whispered, "No, you're not. I don't want you to go either."

"Um, I should probably get going," she whispered. "If I don't, well...I may not go."

Pulling her closer, he told her, "I have something for you and your girls. Hold on just a second."

Walking back to the snowmobile, he removed a box that was tied onto the back of the sled. As he brought it over, he laughed, "Now, I know that you love presents, but you cannot open this until your Christmas Day with Mia and Andi."

"What?" she laughed. "You're going to make me wait?"

"Yes, I am. This is for all three of you, so you cannot do anything until you have your Christmas. When are they coming home?"

"Um…the plan is for them to come back on Friday, so our Christmas morning will be on Saturday. I can't wait. I've missed them," she told him. "I don't know if I will ever get used to having to share them."

"You won't because you are a good parent. Now, let me put this in the back and then you need to get going. I don't like the idea of you driving in the dark," he stated.

"Matt, I've been driving forever and I eat plenty of carrots," she teased.

"Yes, I know, but I'd be happier if you weren't driving such a distance all alone."

"I'll call you when I get back…or send you a text."

Nodding his head, he told her, "You better!"

After getting into the Explorer and buckling her seatbelt, she rolled down her window.

"Matt, I don't know how to tell you how much I've enjoyed this time with you. You saved Christmas for me."

"Jenny, I've thought about you a lot over the years and all I can say is that you are more than I expected. I never expected…well…this," he whispered. Then he gave the top of the vehicle a slap on the top and told her, "Call me when you get home."

As she drove out of the long driveway from camp, she kept glancing in the rearview mirror. She wanted nothing more than to turn around and go back to Matt, but knew it would only delay the inevitable. She had to get back to her life.

Chapter 17

Jenny threw herself down onto her couch and sighed. Everything had been unloaded from the vehicle and she didn't want to move. She'd driven straight through without stopping and she was exhausted.

When she'd brought Mickey in and opened up the carrier, he'd meowed and backed up out of reach. This was very unlike him and all she could think about was how he hadn't wanted to leave his new friend and more than she'd wanted to leave Matt.

Glancing at the clock, she grabbed her cell phone and dialed Matt's number.

"Jenny!" his voice answered. "You home?"

"I am. I just thought I'd let you know I'm home safe," she told him. "Mickey's not so happy about it, though. He hasn't come out of his carrier yet."

"Well, let me tell you. After you left, Minnie and I went back to the house. Before I knew it, she was back over at the cabin. I don't think I'm going to be able to let her out tonight. She's not happy."

Laughing, she said, "It must be the names. They were destined to be together."

"Must be. You know what I realized after you left?"

"What?" she asked quietly. Did he realize he loved her? Like she loved him?

"We never got a puppy picked out for the girls. Do you still want one?"

Okay, so not the answer she was hoping for.

"Yes, but it's okay. I'll find one in a few weeks. Not a biggie," she told him.

"Okay, I just didn't want to disappoint you. Your last few days here, I really didn't want to share you with anyone."

"Yeah, I kind of felt the same way…didn't want to leave the little world we'd created for ourselves at the cabin," she replied. "It was one of the best Christmas' I've ever had."

"For me, too," he said. "Now, I've got to go let the dog out again and keep her leashed this time. Can I call you again, Jenny?"

Jenny's heart fluttered. "Yes. Of course, you can. Anytime."

After hanging up, Jenny got to work and put everything away. By the time she came back into the kitchen where she'd left Mickey's carrier, he'd come out and was now exploring the spot where his food dish was normally kept.

"Yes, Mickey. I will get you some food," and she hurried into the pantry.

The shelves needed to be restocked and after filling Mickey's dish, she grabbed a pen and paper and started making a list. By the time she was finished, she had a full list filled with items including the ingredients for a big dinner and plenty of Christmas cookies.

She only wished that Matt could be there with them and then chided herself for even thinking it. Obviously, there was something between them, but it wouldn't be fair to expect him to conform to here world or the girls to his. It was something that just wouldn't work.

In the meantime, she could enjoy the phone calls and maybe see him every so often. She did plan on taking the girls to camp this summer. She would just have to be satisfied with his friendship and that was that. If only she could make herself believe it.

That night, however, as she curled up in front of the sofa watching television, her cell phone rang and she was delighted and surprised to see Matt's number on the screen.

"Matt!"

"Jenny!" he laughed.

"Sorry, I was just surprised to hear your voice again so soon," she laughed.

"Am I keeping you from anything?" he asked.

Jenny sighed. Should she tell him that since she'd gotten everything put away that she'd done nothing but think about it. No, probably not, she decided.

"No, not all. Just sat down in front of the television, but I couldn't even tell you what's on," she laughed.

"Yeah, I keep mine on for noise, too. Even when I'm working, I need something, but I usually just turn on the radio."

"Me, too. I usually turn it up when the girls are going at it." Ugh, she probably shouldn't have told him that, but she was honest. If the thought of two kids fighting didn't scare him off, nothing would.

She asked, "So, did Minnie try running away again?"

"No, but I kept her right by my side. It's funny how she clicked with you and your cat. Makes me wonder."

"Wonder what?"

"Whether or not we need to take this whole thing more seriously," he laughed. "This you and me and dog and cat thing."

"Are you comparing us to a dog and cat?" she giggled.

"No, well, yeah…kind of," he admitted while laughing.

"I don't know if I should be happy or offended," she teased.

"Well, I would hope it makes you happy," he replied. "Seriously, though, I really enjoyed this Christmas and spending time with you."

"Me, too. Honestly, with all the wine I brought, I think I'd planned on spending it half in the bag," she giggled. "However, thanks to you, I remained sober and I actually had a much better time than I ever thought I could without my kids with me."

"You must be excited to have them come home. Day after tomorrow?"

"Yes and tomorrow I'm working my butt off to get things ready. I've either got to go find a place where I can cut one down or use our fake one."

"Damn, if I had thought about it, I would have cut one down up this way and sent it home to you."

"Yeah, I can just imagine how many needles would have been left on it," she smiled. She could just imagine what the girls would think to come home to a tree without needles and laughed.

"Well, we could have wrapped it," he laughed with her. "I have special powers, you know."

"Special powers?" she asked.

He growled into the phone. "Yes, special powers. You can't tell me you didn't notice?"

Laughing harder, she got up from the couch to get something to drink. "Oh, I noticed a few, but I don't know how they'd have anything to do with keeping needles on a tree."

As she poured a glass of wine, she listened to him tell her about the time that he was six and jumped off the roof because his cousin told him that all he had to do is say three magic words to fly. It was the first broken arm he had of many and his mother had told him that if he didn't stop doing things that the hospital would call child protective services on them.

She'd laughed at the stories he told her and, in return, she'd told him of some of the hair-brained things she'd done as a child.

Three glasses of wine later, she looked at the clock and gasped. "Do you realize it's after midnight?"

"What? Yeah, I guess it is. I'm sorry. I probably kept you long enough," he replied.

"Um, no…I had no plans at all tonight. I already made the shopping list and got it all planned for tomorrow, but I will say goodnight to you. I know you've probably got an early morning."

"Yes, I do, but it's okay. Can I call you tomorrow night?"

"Yes," she told him.

"Goodnight, Sweet Jenny!"

"Goodnight," she whispered.

Chapter 18

Jenny had spent all morning trying to contact one of the Christmas tree farms in her area, hoping that just one would let her in to get a tree. Finally, frustrated to the point that she didn't care anymore, she hopped into the Explorer with her handsaw on the seat beside her.

Five miles later, she'd found her destination. It was a small tree farm and she hoped that a generous donation would allow her on the property.

Knocking on the door, she stood outside in the cold waiting. A few minutes later she knocked again. Two minutes and, if nobody showed up, she was going out to cut one down anyway! She'd leave the money on the door, but she had to have a real tree for the girls.

Just as soon as she turned around to go back down the steps, the door cracked open.

"Can I help you?" The elderly woman peaked out through the crack, the chain on the door still latched.

"Oh, hello! I didn't think anyone was home. I was just wondering if you had any trees left? I can chop it down myself."

"A tree? Christmas is all over, Dear. You're a little late," the woman smiled.

"Oh, I know, but me and my girls had to do our Christmas late this year…divorce and, well…you know. We're doing Christmas on Saturday."

"New Year's Day? That's a funny time to have Christmas," she replied.

"Well, we couldn't help it, but I really want a tree. A nice tree. Not a fake one. Would it be okay if I walked out and cut one down?"

The little old lady unlatched the chain on the door. "You can, Miss, but you can pay me after. Just knock on the door and give me a few minutes. These legs don't get me anywhere too fast these days."

Smiling, Jenny told her, "Absolutely and don't you worry about rushing to the door. I'll wait for you."

Grabbing the saw out of the Explorer, Jenny wandered down into the field and toward the woods. Twenty degrees out with the wind blowing and she was out get ready to saw down a tree. She would have brought an ax, but with her uncanny ability to jinx things, she thought the saw was the safest.

After wandering around, she finally settled on a tree about eight feet in height. Its branches were not perfect, but she could certainly give it a trim. She'd seen better, but she'd seen much worse, too.

She thought about the tree she and Matt had decorated together. The tree had been far from perfect, but in Jenny's eyes, it couldn't have been any more beautiful. They'd laughed as they'd decorated. It was the memories that mattered.

After struggling for almost a half hour with a dull saw, Jenny finally managed to get the tree down and back through the field to the house.

When she leaned it up against her vehicle, she laughed. She probably picked the only lopsided tree on the whole lot.

At the door, she waited a few minutes for the old woman to come to the door. "I'm sorry I took so long. That is the one I picked."

"That?" the elderly woman gasped. "You picked that one?"

"Um, yes…it's fine," she laughed. "Not perfect, but then I'm not either."

"Well, I tell you what. You look like you're half frozen. Come on in for a cup of tea and we can decide on a price."

Jenny smiled. The elderly woman was probably lonely for company. "Tea sounds wonderful."

A few moments later, she was sitting comfortably at the kitchen table with Elizabeth, listening to her talk about how her husband had started the tree farm just before he passed away.

"I am so sorry for your loss. That must have been a difficult time for you," she stated. "How long were you married?"

"Forty-five years, Dear. He's been gone ten years now…doesn't seem possible." Elizabeth cleared her throat and added, "Did I hear you say you were divorced?"

"Yes, I am. This year he got the girls for Christmas. Next year, I'll get them," she replied. "Our first year divorced."

"Well, Dear, I don't know anything about divorce. I was lucky to find my Mr. Right the first time. Maybe you'll meet yours soon," she said while patting Jenny's hand.

"I just recently met someone, but…I don't know. I messed up the first time. I don't want to mess up again."

"Of course, you don't, but if you spend all that time worrying about messing up, you're going to mess up."

Jenny thought about that for a second. "But, if I don't worry, how will I know that he is Mr. Right? Or Mr. Wrong for that matter?"

"Does he make you laugh? Does he do things for you just to make you smile? Is he genuine? These are the questions you have to ask...ask yourself, I mean. Questions are good. It's the answers you got to worry about."

"How did you get so smart?" Jenny laughed.

"Many years of living, Dear. I didn't worry too much about consequences. I followed my heart and look where it led me! Forty-five wonderful years with Frank. I would do anything to have that man back with me, but someday, we'll be together again," Elizabeth smiled.

"I really hope that I can have just a smidgen of the life you had with your husband."

"You can, Jenny. You just have to let go of your inhibitions and let it happen."

"Really? You think that's all?" she asked.

"Yes. Now, I've had a wonderful time chatting with you, but it's almost time for my nap. That's another thing. Take naps. You'll live longer."

Jenny laughed. "I have had such a great time talking to you. Would you mind terribly if I stopped in again sometime for a visit?"

Elizabeth smiled. "That would be wonderful. I don't get out a lot. Darned arthritis acts up too much, especially in this cold weather."

Jenny nodded her head. "That must be tough, but I would love to visit again. Now, how much do you get for your trees?"

"That tree? That tree is free, Dear. We don't sell crooked trees here," Elizabeth stated. "Frank would have a fit if I took your money for that one."

With a promise of another visit, Jenny tied the tree on top of the vehicle and wondered how she would be able to put it up so that the slant would not be so noticeable. Then she laughed at herself for even thinking that it mattered. As long as it sparkled, the girls would love it.

After leaving the tree at home, Jenny went to the grocery store to get everything on the list and, like always, added things onto the list that she'd forgotten, including more wrapping paper that was on discount.

Once home, after putting all of the groceries away, she went on a wrapping spree to wrap the things she made them at camp and the things she'd just purchased. Then, she'd dug through her closet to find the presents she'd already wrapped.

It wasn't until ten that night that she'd realized that Matt hadn't called like he said he would. Should she call him? Then she thought of Elizabeth and her advice. "Lose your inhibitions" she'd been told.

Grabbing her phone, she dialed the number, disappointed that it went to voice mail. Maybe his battery was dead? Maybe he shut it off because he didn't want to talk to her?

Chapter 19

Jenny awoke the next morning at six. After a half a pot of coffee, she finally felt alive enough to start working on Christmas. The girls would be back this afternoon and she wanted everything to be perfect.

The tree gave her the most trouble, but when she finally had secured it to the stand, you couldn't even tell that it was crooked...well, mostly, but that is what made her love it even more.

She thought back to her conversation with Elizabeth and smiled. Maybe someday she would find her Mr. Right, but for right now, she wasn't going to think about it all. At least she was going to try not to.

When the girls arrived at three, they were filled with energy and thrilled that she had not decorated the tree. Kevin laughed as they ran upstairs to their rooms and then gave her a serious look.

"So, who is this Matt?" he asked.

"Just a friend on the lake. I hadn't seen him in years," she replied, hesitant to tell him anymore. The last thing she wanted was a fight.

"Well, I have to say that I didn't like his tactics. You got to Skype with the girls on Christmas, so I expect the same next year."

"You will. Don't worry. So, was Mia any better after I talked to her?" she asked. Anything to get the subject off Matt.

"She was. I won't put up with that type of behavior and she knows it," he stated. "She will get over the divorce or she's going to be miserable. That's her choice."

"Okay, Kevin. Let's just try to make it as easy as possible for her and Andi both."

Before he could say anything else, the girls came running down the stairs.

"Are we going to make cookies?" Mia asked.

Andi whined, "I want hot chocolate!"

"Yes to both, but please say goodbye to your father first," she told them. She didn't want to start anything until he was gone.

A few minutes later, Jenny sat the girls down at the kitchen counter with a cup of hot chocolate and asked, "You had a good time?"

Both nodded their heads. Andi then told her, "We just missed you. I wanted to go with you."

"Oh Sweetie, I missed you, too. We'll have more time next year, but in the meantime we have a lot to do."

It didn't take long for her once-clean kitchen to look like a tornado passed by. Flour was on every surface imaginable, sprinkles crunched under her feet, and everything she touched was sticky. Laughing, Jenny sent the girls upstairs to wash up and change into something clean while she got the kitchen in order.

When her cell phone rang, she dried her hands and answered without looking at the caller ID.

Matt's voice came on the line, "Hello? It sounds like you're happy!"

179

Laughing, she told him, "I don't know why. If you could see the disaster my kitchen is in from cookie making, you'd think I was crazy."

"I bet. Sorry I didn't get to call last night. My Aunt Tilly ended up falling and breaking her hip and I was at the hospital all night."

Jenny gasped, "Is she going to be okay?"

"Yeah, but it will be along recovery for her. The hardest part is her not remembering what happened."

"Well, you give her my love when you see her again. She's a sweet lady."

"Yes, she is and so are you. I missed talking to you. I don't want to keep you on the phone right now...I know your girls need you, but I wanted to say sorry for not calling."

"It's not a problem. We are doing our Christmas Eve tonight and then our Christmas tomorrow morning."

"You haven't opened the package I gave you have you?" he teased.

"No, but I am very curious about it," she giggled. "I can't wait to see it!"

"So, what time do you expect the girls to be awake tomorrow morning? You know all that excitement of opening presents!"

She sighed, "They'll probably wake me up at five, but I won't let them downstairs to start opening presents until seven. I'm a meanie, aren't I?"

"Not at all. My mother made us wait until after breakfast at eight," he told her. "Sitting there staring at the tree while you tried to eat was horrible. We learned not to rush, though, because we had to wait until my parents finished theirs, too."

"Okay, so I'm not that mean, then?" she laughed.

"Nope. The girls will appreciate it when they're older. Well, you have a fun evening with them and I will give you a call tomorrow."

Jenny didn't want to hang up, but she also didn't want to keep the girls waiting any longer. "Sounds good. I'll talk to you tomorrow."

To the girls, she yelled, "Who's ready to make pizza?"

Screeches of excitement came from the living room and they soon appeared in the doorway. Of course, that only lasted until Mia tried telling Andi that she shouldn't put so many pepperonis on the pizza or it would be too greasy. As she listened to them fighting, she could only smile. She'd missed this!

It wasn't until that they were all tucked into bed that she finally sat down and thought about Matt. Poor Aunt Tilly! Bad enough that she had Alzheimer's and then to break a hip. Knowing Matt he'd stay right by her side. That was one of the reasons she loved him.

Her thoughts made her gasp. She did love him! Her hands shook as the realization hit her full on. She didn't have to keep searching for Mr. Right! She'd already met him!

Now, she just had to figure out a way to let him know how she felt and, with any luck, he'd feel the same way about her.

She'd never been more scared in her life and, after getting the presents all under the tree, she was awake for hours wondering if he could possibly feel the same way about her.

Chapter 20

Jenny could barely open her eyes at six-thirty when Mia and Andi came bounding into the room and jumped on her bed.

"Mama! It's Christmas again! You have to wake up!" Andi yelled while bouncing on her.

"Don't jump on my bladder or I'll pee my pants," she giggled and pulled Andi closer.

Mia curled up beside her and whispered, "I missed you, Mama."

Pulling the two of them into her arms, Jenny smiled. "I missed you both. Now, let's relax a few minutes before we get up. How about seven?"

"Seven? That's hours away!" Andi whined.

"No, it's not, Stupid. It's only thirty minutes," Mia snapped.

Andi started to cry, "She called me stupid!"

Jenny sat up in bed. "Okay, Mia, be nice to your sister and Andi, calm down. Why don't you watch television for a minute while I go to the bathroom and brush my teeth? Then, we'll go downstairs."

After taking her time in the bathroom, she stepped back into the room to find both of the girls had fallen back to sleep. Slipping out of the room, she went downstairs to turn on the tree lights and start the coffee.

Back upstairs, she stepped into the room and leaned over the girls snuggled in her bed. Mia had grown so much and was turning into a beautiful young woman. Andi, just two years younger, still held on to the chubby cheeks she'd had since she was a baby. It was hard to believe that both would be in their teens soon.

Mia stirred and opened her eyes, "Is it time?"

Nodding her head, Jenny leaned over and hugged Andi. "Time to get up, Sleepyhead."

Seconds later, she laughed as they raced out of the room and downstairs. Screeches of delight filled her ears and she laughed. This made everything worth it.

"Wait just a minute! Don't open up any of those presents until I start handing them out," she laughed.

About half way through the presents, the doorbell rang and Jenny glanced at the clock. Who would be knocking this early? It better not be Kevin interrupting our Christmas, she thought. He had his time and this was hers.

When she opened the door, she just about fell over in shock. Thankfully, her hand on the doorknob held her up. She couldn't even say anything. Just stood there with her mouth hanging open.

Matt's laughter broke the spell. In his arms, he held a chocolate colored, curly-haired puppy that kept trying to lick his chin. "Merry Christmas!" he laughed. "I hope you don't mind me just showing up, but I had this gift from Santa for two special little girls."

Jenny couldn't do anything but laugh. "You came all this way? Oh my God, Matt! Really? You got them a puppy?"

"No, Santa did. Do you mind if we come in? It's a little chilly out here." The smile on his face was more than she could take and, before letting him in, she reached up to kiss him only to find a puppy tongue lapping at her mouth.

"Oh my! You are a cute thing, aren't you?" she cooed.

When Matt stepped in, he asked, "Are the girls up?"

"Yes, they are opening presents right now. Follow me," she whispered.

When she entered the room, both girls were checking out the gifts they had already opened and didn't even notice Matt behind them. It wasn't until the puppy let out a bark that they looked up.

Andi screeched, "A puppy! You got us a puppy?"

Mia, a little more reserved, looked at Matt and asked, "Who are you? Is that your puppy?"

Matt spoke, "Well, it's like this. Santa knew you weren't having Christmas with your mom until today, so he left this little girl in my care until this morning. She doesn't have a name yet, so that's one of the first things you will want to do."

Mia looked at her mother with tears in her eyes, "Really? A puppy?"

Andi had walked right up to Matt and asked, "Can I hold her?"

Laughing, Jenny told the girls. "Yes, it's a puppy for you both. There will be no fighting over her. She is not a toy and you will have to take care of her. Can you both agree to that?"

Both girls cried, "Yes!" and Matt set her down on the floor.

The puppy promptly walked over to the tree and squatted down to pee. Jenny and Matt looked at each other and laughed, which sent the girls into a giggling fit.

After cleaning up the mess and opening the rest of the gifts, Jenny pulled out the box from Matt. "Okay, girls. This one is for all of us from Matt."

The girls tore into the box and found everything needed for their new puppy, including a small bag of dogfood, a brush, a collar, and a leash. There was also a book about taking care of puppies and several toys. The girls both ran up and gave him a hug and Jenny felt herself falling even more.

It wasn't until after the girls took their presents upstairs that she had a chance to talk to him alone.

"Why, Matt? Why would you do this? I don't even know what to say," she whispered.

Matt put his arms around her and held her close. "I just wanted you and the girls to be happy, Jenny. That's all. No repayment needed, unless…unless you want to give me a kiss," he teased.

Jenny put her arms around his neck and pulled him closer. When her lips touched his, he held her tighter and his lips responded swiftly. When she heard the girl's voices in the background, she quickly let him go.

"I'm…I don't know…I was shocked to find you on my doorstep. I'm still shocked that you are here," she said.

"I know and I'm sorry. I didn't want to spoil the surprise. I gave my Aunt a call and asked if she would mind a visitor for a couple of days."

"So you are here for a few days?" She couldn't believe it.

"I am. Of course, I want to spend some time with my Aunt Elizabeth, too, but I will have plenty of free time for you. You know what's funny? My Aunt Elizabeth had someone show up yesterday for a tree and she said she gave them a crooked tree…wouldn't take any money for it. Looks to me like your tree is a little crooked," he laughed.

"Elizabeth is your aunt? Really?" Jenny laughed. It really was a small world.

"Yes, she is my mother's sister. She spoke very highly of you," he told her. "She wants me to take a picture of your tree."

"Oh, a picture isn't good enough. Would you and your Aunt like to join us for Christmas dinner? We're having ham and all the fixings. The girls and I made cookies and I know you'll love the pie."

"Are you sure we wouldn't be imposing? I know you missed your time with the girls."

"Absolutely not. You brought them a puppy," she laughed. "They won't have a problem with you being here and I can guarantee they will love your aunt as much as I do."

"Can I be honest with you, Jenny?" Matt asked seriously.

"Of course!"

"I don't know if it's possible or not, but Jenny, I swear I fell in love with you the moment I saw you standing outside the camp when I came looking for Minnie. Am I crazy?"

Laughing, Jenny threw herself into his arms. "God, I hope not, Matt. Otherwise, it means I'm crazy, too."

Just then, the puppy ran into the room with the girls following closely behind. Laughing, the puppy found the dish of cat food and proceeded to wolf it down.

Mia was the one to stand up and take the dish away. She then scolded the puppy, "No, you need to listen. That's Mickey's dish and if you want him to like you, you won't eat his food."

Both Matt and Jenny started laughing and Matt asked, "Did you guys decide on a name yet?"

Mia looked at the puppy and teased, "Trouble?"

Andi asked, "How about Christmas?"

Matt leaned over and told her, "That's a great idea. You could call her Chrissy for short! How does that sound Mia? Jenny?"

Mia giggled, "I like it! Come here, Chrissy!"

Chrissy let out a bark and ran in the opposite direction, sending them all into another fit of giggles.

"Well, I don't know if she liked it or not, but I think it suits her," Jenny laughed. "Now, we got to clean up this mess. Mia and Andi, you don't mind if Matt and his Aunt Elizabeth join us for dinner, do you?"

"Yay! Matt's going to stay," Andi yelled and went screeching up the stairs.

Mia went up to Matt and told him, "Do you like cookies?"

Matt patted his belly and said, "Of course!"

Chapter 21

Jenny placed the ham on the table and looked around and smiled. Matt sat beside Andi and across the table, Mia sat beside Elizabeth. She still couldn't believe that Elizabeth was his aunt and what a coincidence it had been to have already met her.

As she sat down at the head of the table, Jenny asked them all, "Does anyone want to say Grace?"

Matt responded, "If you don't mind, I would love to."

Everyone took hands and bowed their heads.

"Dear Lord, I cannot thank you enough for sending these wonderful people into my life. We celebrate today in honor of Jesus, but we also celebrate family, friends, and love and laughter. We thank you for the food on this table. In the name of Jesus, Amen."

Jenny felt her eyes burning with unshed tears. She really did have so much to be thankful for, even if Matt hadn't come into her life.

Andi interrupted her thoughts by asking, "Mom, can I have pie first?"

Jenny laughed. "No, you may not. Pie is for after you eat everything else."

As the ham, potatoes, stuffing, and vegetables made the rounds about the table, she watched as Matt helped Andi to get food on her plate. He was a natural. Kevin always expected her to take care of both girls while he started his meal.

Once dinner was over, things once again became chaotic when Mickey came out of his hiding spot to meet the newest member of the family.

He sniffed as he circled the puppy, his hair standing on end. Matt told the girls to stay back and let them get acquainted. This turned out to be sound advice, as Chrissy decided Mickey was play toy and lunged. Within seconds,

Chrissy was chasing Mickey and neither cared who was in the way.

Laughing, Matt asked his Aunt Elizabeth if she was ready to go home and she nodded to her head.

To Jenny, she said, "I can't thank you enough for including me and allowing me to see the tree. That old crooked thing looks terrific."

"You are so welcome, Elizabeth. I'm so happy you could join us. I was so shocked to find out you were Matt's Aunt," she laughed.

Elizabeth leaned toward Jenny and whispered, "Just remember what I told you. Lose the inhibitions and you'll get Mr. Right!"

Glancing at Matt first to make sure he hadn't heard, she told Elizabeth, "I will. Thank you!"

Later on that evening, the girls had already been tucked into bed, tired out from the day of activities, Jenny put a bottle of wine on to chill and got out two glasses of wine.

Matt had called and said he'd be running a little late as he'd gotten caught up talking to his cousin. At eight o'clock, the doorbell rang and Jenny smiled.

Lose her inhibitions? She sure hoped she could. It had been so long that she'd let her guard down, she wasn't sure it was even possible anymore.

However, when Matt walked into the kitchen and swept her up into his arms, she lost all her concerns. This was just what she needed.

After setting her back down on the floor, Matt laughed. "I'm sorry. I missed you."

"I can see that," she giggled. "Now, do you want to go for a walk in the cold with me? I've got to let Miss Chrissy outside before she decides to pee on the floor again."

"Uh, I'm sorry. The joys of potty training a puppy. Why don't you let me do that for you while you pour us a glass of wine? As cold as it is out there, she should go pretty quickly."

"You know, I'm going to let you do that," she giggled. "Now, let me just find her. She's probably back under the tree chewing on something she's not supposed to."

Jenny was right and found the puppy right where she thought she would…chewing on one of her slippers. "No, we don't chew," she scolded. "It's really a good thing you are cute and so sweet. However, I think we named you wrong. Your name should be Tara!"

Matt, who had heard the whole conversation, could only laugh. "Come on, Chrissy," he said while emphasizing her name. "Time to go pee. You want to go out? Out?"

To Jenny, he said, "If you teach her the word out first, she will automatically associate it with going pee. I'm no expert dog trainer, but it does work."

"I'll remember that," she told him. "Now, hurry back in and I will pour the wine."

When Matt came stomping back through the door ten minutes later, he stated, "Pee'd and pooped. Hopefully, she will be good for the night. Where is she sleeping tonight?"

Jenny looked around. "Oh, I didn't even think about that. What do you think?"

Looking around the room, he told her, "Well, the best option would be a dog crate. Damn, I wish I would have thought about it. I would have picked you up one. However, do you have a big box?"

Jenny nodded her head and went out into the garage. Within minutes, she was back inside with a big box. She also grabbed an old blanket and laid it out on the bottom. Placing the box in the kitchen, she asked, "Do you think she will be okay here?"

Matt surveyed the box and its location. "It's perfect. She'll be fine and you won't have to listen to her whine while you're trying to sleep. I'll let her out one more time before I leave, too. Maybe she'll sleep later that way."

Jenny smiled. "How can I ever thank you for everything you've done?"

"Jenny, you don't need to thank you. I'm just happy to actually see you. The few days you were gone were…I don't know…awful," he laughed. "What are we going to do?"

Jenny handed him a glass of wine, picked up hers, and led him into the living room. They sat down on the couch, side by side.

Matt put his wine glass down on the coffee table and turned to her. "Okay. Here are my thoughts, however chaotic they may be. I fell hard for you and I want to see where it goes."

Jenny nodded her head. "I feel the same way. I've just been going back and forth on how we can make this work…we live so far away from each other."

Matt took her hand in his. "I know and that's been my biggest worry, but let's not worry about that right now."

Jenny nodded her head. When she heard Chrissy whine out in the kitchen, she went to stand up. "No, it's okay. She has to learn that someone isn't going to come whenever she whines. She'll be fine for a few minutes."

Jenny sat back down on the couch. "You should have seen me when the girls were little. I jumped whenever they made a sound," she laughed.

"I wish things were different…that we'd met sooner. But, we can't pass up on what we have because we don't live closer to one another. What do you think about coming up to the lake every other weekend? And every other weekend I can come down this way?"

Jenny thought about it. She'd talked a lot about getting the girls at camp more and she knew that her mother would be thrilled that the camp would actually get used.

"Um, we should be able to do that. It might be hard during the colder months…you know, if it is storming, but I can commit to that," she told him.

"Yes, no driving in storms. We'll figure that out as we go along. I work when I want to work…when I have inspiration, so I can come down during the week sometimes, too. We'll make this work."

He'd thought of everything. They would see each other a lot, according to him and, well…she suddenly felt panicked. After all of this planning, what if it didn't work? What if he decided he didn't love her anymore? Like Kevin did?

"Jenny, are you okay?" he asked. She couldn't even answer him...she didn't know what to say.

"I know you're nervous," he told her. "After all, you have the girls..."

Cutting him off, she stood up quickly, "Um, I don't know, Matt. This just seems so quick...so fast...I don't know."

Jenny took a deep breath. "I think I just need time. Do you mind calling it a night?"

Matt stood up and pulled her close. "I'm sorry, Jenny. I just don't want to lose you. I'm shocked by the whole thing, too, but I think you're worth fighting for."

It wasn't until Matt left that Jenny sat down on the couch and cried. How could she do this to the girls again? It wouldn't last with Matt. No matter what he said, she would do something to screw it up, the same way that she had done with Kevin. She wouldn't do it to the girls again.

Chapter 22

It had been a week and Jenny could still not get her act together. She cried at the drop of a hat and was crabby to the girls. They'd gone back to school and it was all she could do to keep her mind on work. Her thoughts were on Matt and all of his text and calls that she'd ignored.

She hadn't meant to hurt him. She just knew she was saving them a lot of hurt down the road. Now, it was Friday night and the girls were at their father's for the weekend. Unfortunately, it just gave her more time to think.

How sad was it that she'd even tried to switch weekends with Kevin just so she didn't have to be alone?

She thought about going out to the movies, but it was cold out and she just didn't have the energy. She thought about grabbing a book to read, but knew she wouldn't be able to concentrate. The only thing left do was to sit down in front of the television and have a glass of wine.

After pulling out a bottle of wine, she sat down on the couch and hesitated in pouring herself a glass. Hell, if she was going to make it through the weekend, she'd have to find a better way than to get drunk.

She really didn't drink often, but the thought of waking up tomorrow with a headache just put her in a worse mood.

The television didn't offer much to amuse her, either. She was not going to waste time on love stories…she'd already cried enough. The cooking shows just mocked her. Instead, she put it on the news and decided to put the wine back and make coffee instead. So what if it kept her awake! It wasn't like she was sleeping well anyways.

Just as she entered the kitchen, a knock sounded at the door and Chrissy let out a bark. If anything, the puppy was proving that she would be a good guard dog when she grew up.

Opening the door, she found Matt on the steps.

"Before you say anything, let me speak. Please?"

"Matt. I'm…"

"Please, Jenny?" he asked as he took a step forward. She stepped back and allowed him in.

"I won't keep you long, but I have to tell you that I'm sorry."

Jenny interrupted. "Sorry? You have nothing to be sorry for. It's me, Matt. I'm broken. I've thought about this all week. It's not you…it's me."

Matt took off his coat. "You know, you are seriously wrong. No matter what you say, I know you love me. I know I came on too strong. It's not you, Jenny."

A tear slid down her cheek and she reached and wiped it away before Matt could see it.

"Okay, just come in and make yourself comfortable. I…was just…I don't know…"

Matt steered her into the living room. "Jenny, will you please just let me talk," he laughed.

Jenny sat and shut up. Inside she was starting to fume. What gave him the right to order her around? This was her house!

"Jenny, I know we have something. I've said it once and I will say it again. I love you. Yes, it happened quickly, and I wouldn't change it for the world."

Chrissy came up and started chewing on a bone at his feet. As he reached down to pet her, he continued. "I was so infatuated when we were teenagers. Your grandmother scared me away. I told you that. But what I didn't tell you is that I finally got her approval only to find out you were dating Kevin. I was going to ask you out, but I decided not to."

Getting up from the couch, he began to pace. "I spent a lot of time at your camp with your parents after you started dating him. Your father was never happy that Kevin kept you away from family. He understood it, but he wasn't happy."

Jenny was shocked. Her parents had never told her that Matt had come over to visit with them. Even now, her mother had not said a thing when she'd gotten back from camp and found out that she and Matt had spent Christmas together.

"You know, I never got you out of my head. Even when I got married. It wasn't fair to her to get married when my heart was someplace else, but I thought you were happy. I wanted to be happy to."

Jenny spoke up. "I didn't know, Matt."

"No, you didn't, Jenny, but now you do. I'm not some lovesick teenager anymore. Neither are you. We're adults and we can't let a second chance pass us by."

As the tears rolled down her cheeks, Jenny stood up. "I'm sorry, Matt. I'm just…scared, I guess."

Matt's voice rose. "I'm scared, too, but that's a good sign. Hell, I'd follow you anywhere. If you are worried about a long-distance relationship, don't. I'll move down this way. All you have to do is say yes to giving us a chance."

Jenny couldn't believe it. Matt loved her enough that he'd change his whole life for her? She knew he cared, but to give up everything he'd worked so hard for...no. She couldn't let him. It wouldn't be fair and he'd end up resenting her later on.

"No, Matt. You don't have to do that, but I want this. I just...I don't know how to get past feeling scared," she whispered.

Matt came to her side and wrapped his arms around her. "We'll figure it out. I just don't want to lose you, Jenny."

"I don't want to lose you, either," she cried. "This week has been awful. I missed you so much!"

"I thought I'd lost you when you didn't answer my texts or calls."

"I'm sorry, Matt. I thought it was for the best."

"Well, you can thank my Aunt Elizabeth. She came right out and told me that if I thought you were worth fighting for that I'd get my butt back here and win you over," he laughed.

Jenny giggled. "Did I tell you how much I love your aunt?"

"You don't have to, but you can tell me how much you love me?" he whispered.

"I love you, Matt," she whispered, but she didn't think he heard her because his lips were too busy doing fabulous things to her own.

"What time are the girls coming home?" he asked.

Giggling, she teased, "Sunday. You got plans for the weekend?"

"Only to make you fall in love with me even more," he whispered as he picked her up in her arms to take her upstairs.

Epilogue

Jenny looked down at the sleeping infant and smiled. Swaddled in blue, Matthew James Gray II slept peacefully. This surprised her with all of the noise surrounding them.

Matt's parents were hosting another one of their Christmas' and this year there were more people than the last. In fact, it was the first year that Mia and Andi were here and from what she could tell, they were having a blast.

Aunt Elizabeth and her son, Tom and his family had even joined them this year. Elizabeth had spent the first hour holding on to Matthew and talking with the girls. It was funny to think that she and Elizabeth had lived so close and never gotten to know each other until just after she met Matt.

Glancing at the clock, she realized it was almost feeding time for Matthew and picked him up to take him upstairs. Matt's mother had told her the sewing room had a comfortable chair where she could feed him in private.

When Matt saw where she was headed, he leaned down and spoke to the girls and quickly followed behind.

After helping her get situated in the room, he sat down and watched as she guided her nipple into Matthew's mouths. It took him a bit, but soon the suckling sound filled the room.

With a smile, she looked up at Matt's face who was watching with an intense gaze. "I still can't believe he's here already," she whispered.

Matthew had just been born two weeks before, about a month ahead of schedule. He was small, but healthy.

Matt leaned over and kissed the top of his son's head. "I still can't believe I have a son."

Jenny smiled. Life had a certain way of changing quickly. It was only three years ago that she had gone to Moosehead Lake for Christmas and since then, life had been a whirlwind of changes.

They'd gotten married less than a year after they had rediscovered each other and she and the girls had moved to Moosehead Lake permanently.

Kevin, her ex-husband, was now remarried to June, a woman that treated both of the girls wonderfully. She couldn't believe how well she and Kevin got along now. Of course, she also knew that Matt had a great deal to do with that. If Kevin got out of line, Matt would step right up and let him know it wasn't acceptable and usually, Kevin's wife was right there to back Matt up.

Co-parenting wasn't always easy, but with Matt and June's assistance, it was a lot better than she could have ever expected.

The hardest part had been figuring out visitation with the girls. Living five hours from their father's house wasn't exactly conducive to quick visits during the week. However, the girls Skyped with him almost daily and went to visit him every other weekend, with either she or Matt providing the rides.

As she switched sides, Matthew let out a wail and Matt laughed. "I love the sounds he makes."

"Well, tell me that in about another month. He's still new," she giggled. "I'm just hoping that he stays this easy."

"I know, but when you start pumping, at least I can help out with the feedings."

At that moment, Mia and Andi came into the room.

"Yeah, I think I'm going to have to be referee and keep you all from fighting over who is going to feed him when he starts on the bottle. We'll have to create a schedule," she stated.

Mia stood in front of her mother, hands on her hips. "Can I hold him after?"

Andi whined, "But I wanted to take him downstairs and show him off."

Matt stood up and told the girls, "No, your job today is to go have fun. We'll be going outside soon for the bonfire. You want to dress warm."

With excitement in their steps, they took off, leaving Matt and Jenny alone with Matthew.

"Jenny, how can I ever thank you? I still cannot believe that all of this…I mean, all of us…I guess what I am trying to say is that I can't believe that we have all of this after three years."

"I know. It's crazy. I am just so thankful that we have this little guy here with us this year. What a great present," she said as she nuzzled her son's neck.

"Yes, but I have to say that Christmas three years ago was one for the books. Never did I expect to fall in love so quickly or so hard," Matt told her.

Jenny smiled. She remembered almost letting him go because she was scared that he would one day let her go. Since then, Matt had proven over and over again how much he loved her.

His Aunt Elizabeth had also played a big part in their relationship. She and her husband had forty-five years of happiness together and Jenny knew that she and Matt could easily match that if given the time.

"I'm sorry I gave you such a hard time at the beginning," she giggled. "I can't believe I acted so stupid."

"Not stupid. You were looking out for you and your daughters. I can't blame you for that. I'm just happy that Aunt Elizabeth pushed me in to coming back to see you."

"Pushed? You mean you weren't going to come back on your own?" Jenny asked.

"Not at the point, but if she would have given me a few days, I would have figured it out on my own. I may have gone too fast with our relationship, but I can be slow at times," he laughed.

"No, I think you're perfect," she laughed. "Maybe a little slow at some things, but I like it that way."

"Watch it or we could end up with another little one," he murmured.

Looking at Matt's face, she'd never dreamed that she could be so happy. Little Matthew had been quite the surprise for both of them. Being over forty, having another child had been the last thing she'd expected. Matt had called it fate. She called it destiny.

"Merry Christmas," she whispered just before Matt's lips met hers.

Dear Reader:

Thank you so much for taking the time to read *Christmas at Moosehead Lake*. I hope you enjoyed reading it as much as I enjoyed writing it for you!

I have a lot of fond memories of the Moosehead Lake region and, if you are ever in Maine, it is the one place that you need to put on your list to visit.

I love to hear from readers and you can find me on Facebook:
https://www.facebook.compennyharmonauthor
or you can email me at
pennyharmonauthor@gmail.com.

Thank you again and happy reading!

Penny Harmon

CPSIA information can be obtained
at www.ICGtesting.com
Printed in the USA
LVOW13s0025161216
517517LV00008B/124/P